BODIES OF EVIDENCE

A. S. FRENCH

NEONOIR BOOKS

ALSO BY A. S. FRENCH

Crime Fiction and Thrillers

The Astrid Snow series

Book one: Don't Fear the Reaper

Book two: The Killing Moon

Book three: Lost in America

Book four: Gone to Texas

Book five: The Final Girl

The Ophelia Red series

Book one: Ophelia Red

The Detective Jen Flowers series

Book one: The Hashtag Killer

Book two: Serial Killer

Book three: Night Killer

Book four: The Killer Inside Them

The Frank Walker series

Where The Bodies Are Buried

Crime Short Stories

Call Me: An Astrid Snow Short Story

Dark Snow: An Astrid Snow Short Story

Bette Davis Eyes: Detective Flowers Short Story

Writing as Andrew. S. French

Science Fiction

The Time Traveller's Murder

The Mercy Sleep

Bodies

The Arcane Supernatural Thriller Series

Book one: The Arcane

Book two: The Arcane Identity

Book three: The Arcane Quest

Book four: The Arcane Ultimatum

The Ella Finn Fantasy Novella Series

Ella and the Elementals

Ella and the Multiverse

Ella and the Monsters

Ella and the Dreamers

Supernatural Short Stories

Dead Souls

The Shadow

Go to www.andrewsfrench.com for more information.

1 THE UPSIDE DOWN

It was a hell of a way to kill a man.

Carrying the body wasn't easy. Even with the chemicals in their blood, they'd still wriggle around. And the heavier they were, the more awkward it was. The first one kept going wrong, the arms flailing, flopping, and proving a nuisance. He knocked a table over, sending porcelain figures crashing everywhere, Mickey Mouse's ears flapping over Betty Boop's exaggerated bosom. The victim's eyes glazed over, lips trembling as gloved hands dragged him past the cracked head of Queen Elizabeth II. He wanted to scream, to shout, as the gloves hauled him towards the wall.

It was cold in the room, replicating the insides of a fridge, but his skin burnt as his captor lifted him onto their shoulder. He clawed at his abductor's face, reaching out for the eyes while struggling to see who had drugged him. The air smelt of rotten wood as he tried to speak, the words stumbling over his lips and dying a second later. He mumbled a protest and wriggled his hips. A swarm of bees buzzed inside his head as his vision cleared, realising he was still in his house as his captor dumped him against the wall. He slumped into it, watching as a blurry face peered into his. Then he heard the voice crawling over his skin like a slug.

'We think we have forever, believing we're immortal, even though all the evidence says otherwise. Each day is nothing but a litany of events designed to trick us into thinking our lives are significant: work, rest and play to keep reality away. We've got eternity, but we don't do anything with it. Until now.'

'What?' the victim said.

The reply fizzed in the air like an out-of-tune radio station.

'Did you know the Persians invented crucifixion three or four hundred years before Christ was crucified? It developed, during Roman times, into a punishment for the most serious criminals?' The fuzz in his head made it impossible to identify if it was a man or woman talking to him. 'And you're a most serious criminal.'

This wasn't an ordinary crucifixion because he had to be upside down as the nails went through his wrists and ankles. So that added to the complications, especially as he kept slipping down the wall like a drunken marionette.

He lay slumped beside the skirting board as his captor left the room. One trembling hand reached out to drag his body up, finding cobwebs, and the smell of yesterday's spilt milk. His spine ached as he peered at the ceiling, and his abductor looked for the solution to the problem of keeping the body against the wall. Then he gazed at those broken porcelain figures, admiring Charlie Chaplin's hat while staring into Louise Brook's magnetic eyes.

It was five minutes of searching the house to find the answer – thick black tape to prevent him from moving too much, though it took a long time to get his legs pushed up to the wall and his head in the correct position so he wouldn't fall. A strategically placed knee in the chest helped with that. However, one of his ribs cracked because of the pressure. He groaned in pain through the haze of the ketamine, but that would be the least of his worries – soon, it would be suffocation, loss of body fluids and multiple organ failures.

The tape kept his legs upright and in place as the intruder drilled the nails through the ankles and into the wall. The electric drill let out a shrill vibration as it punched through sinew and bone. More agony surged through him, a rollercoaster of despair running up and down every inch; only the gag prevented his screams from filling the room.

Once the feet were secure, it was easy to do the rest. The ketamine may have lessened some initial pain, which was an unfortunate but necessary side effect. In time, the heart and lungs would stop working as the blood drained through the wounds, but the agony would last long enough. Someone nailed to a crucifix with their arms stretched out on either side could expect to live for no more than twenty-four hours, but this was different since they were upside down. Then, it was up to the bones in the feet to support the body's weight.

Now, suspended at their ankles, the torso hung downward rather than from their wrists. The intestines compressed the lungs and diaphragm, but it would asphyxiate him far slower than folding the abdomen on them. He would be in agony from the blood's gravitation into the head's blood vessels and from the body's weight driving his head into an awkward posture against the ground. Blood pooling in the veins and arteries of the skull kept him conscious for a while, meaning that light-headedness didn't detract from his awareness of the pain.

It was an arduous process that took a long time but was worth the trouble.

And it made the ones that followed so much easier.

2 ON THE BEACH

My arms throbbed as I pushed the old man across the sand. The wind and the sun competed for my attention, with the smell of the sea drifting over me. A flock of gulls squawked nearby, and my father chuntered at them. My breathing was long and laboured as the sweat covered my forehead.

'Whose idea was it to take a wheelchair onto the beach?'

He popped the false teeth into his mouth to grin at me.

'That would be you, Frank. Now, where are the fish and chips you promised me?'

I stopped gazing at the fishing boats trawling for the day's catch. It was hotter than the inside of Chernobyl, so I was glad to be wearing shorts and a t-shirt. And thankful for the sea breeze blowing across my face. My father fidgeted in the seat, in his shirt and suit as if he was going to a wedding. Or a funeral.

He rubbed at a neck that was nothing but wrinkles and smiled at me. I should have been happy in the sun but thoughts of death consumed me. Only this morning, he'd told me he wanted to be cremated. I'd burnt the toast while making breakfast, and the smell must have made him think about his imminent future.

'You can keep my ashes on top of the TV in the living room,' he said. I only nodded in reply, reluctant to engage in that conversation.

As a general rule of thumb, the younger you die, the better the turnout for a funeral. So the dream is to expire at ninety-eight with nobody at the crematorium apart from a couple of stragglers who have turned up for the wrong person. Last week, I'd taken my father to the memorial of one of his drinking buddies from the pub. There was a crowd of dozens, and the church was packed. I wasn't the only person to observe that I'd have to pay to get so many for my funeral.

I pushed that thought from my head. I'd promised him a trip to the beach and fish and chips after his latest round of tests at the hospital's memory clinic. His dementia was getting worse, and the doctors told me it was only a matter of time before he'd need daily professional support. A nurse had asked me if other family members could help with his care, but I said there was only me. I didn't feel like telling them I hadn't seen either of my two sisters in decades or that my older brother was in prison for murder.

'I understand you're a former police officer,' Dr Carlisle said to me at the hospital.

She had eyes bluer than the sea, with a siren's voice, and was the only reason to look forward to those trips to Ward 13. It felt wrong to ask her on a date, but I was still building courage after four visits.

I returned that smile, hoping it was as warm as hers was. 'I was a detective inspector.'

I didn't mention working for the Metropolitan Police since the Met had a terrible reputation. Dr Carlisle turned from looking at my father's medical records on the computer and stared at me. Her pristine white uniform resurrected fantasies I'd had as a teenager of doctors and nurses.

'It must be quite a culture shock for you, Mr Walker, living in the north compared to London's bright lights and glamour.'

I had to still my beating heart. 'There are plenty of attractions here, Dr Carlisle.' I cringed as the words came out of my mouth. 'And please call me Frank.'

She laughed at me. 'Yes, your father said you were taking him to the beach this afternoon. It's not exactly the Riviera, but we have the best fish and chips in the world.'

So we were waiting for the food and I still hadn't asked her for a date. And I didn't know her first name. My father must have been reading my mind.

'You fancy my doctor, don't you?'

Gulls swooped overhead, and I expected them to crap on me at any second.

'Which one?'

His laugh resembled air rushing out of a recently opened sarcophagus.

'The bloke looking like a boxer who's never won a fight, obviously.'

'I'm far too old for him, Dad.'

His teeth rattled as he laughed. 'Wait until you get to my age, Frank, and then you'll know what old is.'

I laughed with him, so I didn't hear the third person in our party approach.

'I drowned yours in vinegar, as you asked, Jack.'

Lydia handed my father his food. The smell rushed up to my nose and made my head spin. She gave me my fish and chips and I thanked her while peering at her clothes: a large jumper, scarf, and tight leggings, on one of the hottest days of the year. She ignored my gaze and funnelled chips into her mouth as she sat on the sand. She'd spent a month travelling around North Africa, so everywhere here was never warm enough for her now.

'Don't eat too fast,' I said to my father as he munched on a giant piece of batter. I kept giving him advice on healthy living, though at ninety-three, with a failing body and even worse memory, I wasn't sure why I was doing it.

Lydia threw a chip into the air and the gulls swooped down to fight over it.

'How did it go at the hospital?'

'The usual,' I said as I watched the old man down his grub like a little kid.

'Have you given any more thought about Jack going into a residential care home?'

I grabbed Lydia's arm and dragged her away from my father.

'Don't let him hear you say that. I'm not putting him somewhere to die with strangers.'

She frowned at me. 'He might live for another five years, while his memory and body get worse. And you're in no fit state to give him the care he needs.'

'What do you mean no fit state?'

She wriggled from my grasp. 'Look at you, Frank. I was only away a month and you've gone to seed: your hair's a mess, you haven't shaved in weeks, and a couple of extra pounds of blubber are sticking out of those shorts. Kitty must have been impressed when you arrived at the hospital looking like that.'

'Kitty?'

Lydia threw more chips into the sand. 'Dr Kitty

Carlisle. I've heard you have a little crush on the poor woman.'

I glanced at my father, seeing the bits of fish clinging to his chin and worried that a gull might fly down to snatch them from his face. Visions of Alfred Hitchcock's *The Birds* filled my head.

'You heard wrong.' I went to the old man and cleaned him up. 'Would you like an ice cream, Dad?'

He beamed at me as if he was a child on Christmas Day. 'I'd prefer a pint of cider.'

I had a sudden urge for a drink as well.

'Okay. We can sit outside the pub across the road.' I looked at Lydia. 'Are you coming with us?'

She shrugged. 'Sure. What young woman doesn't want to spend her afternoon with a slob and his old man?'

I grabbed the wheelchair and pushed it through the sand.

'If you have better things to do, Lydia, don't let us stop you.'

She walked by my side. 'We could all go to the prison to visit our relatives.'

I grimaced at her. 'Have you been to see your uncle Tony since returning from Africa?'

'Once or twice. Have you visited your brother?'

I shook my head. 'Why would I, considering what he did?'

My arms throbbed from pushing the wheelchair, and the sweat was now a river in my hair. We crossed the road and headed to the nearest pub. Across the way, I saw a crowd gathering outside the new community centre, remembering it was today's official opening. We'd get a good view of the ceremony while we had our refreshments. I still tasted fish in my mouth and looked forward to the sweet cider washing it away.

Lydia sat at the nearest table. 'Families should stick together no matter what. He's still your brother, Frank.'

I didn't want to think about that, leaving the old man at the table and going inside for the drinks. When I returned with three pints of cider, Lydia and he were whispering like conspirators planning a bank robbery.

'What are you two talking about?'

Lydia smiled at me. 'We were discussing the impossible task of trying to make you attractive to the opposite sex.' She took her drink. 'Or to anybody, really.'

I slumped in the seat, sipping on the cider and hoping it might cool me down.

'What about you?' I said. 'Did you meet anybody special on your travels?'

'By special, are you asking if I was romantically involved with anyone?'

The heat warming my cheeks wasn't from the sun or the alcohol.

'Eh, yeah, I suppose I was.'

She grinned at me. 'You're not my dad, Frank.'

Before I could reply, there was a roar from nearby, and I turned to see the people gathered outside the new community centre.

'Are the Germans bombing us again?' my father said.

'No, Dad.' I explained to him what was happening. 'It's been over thirty years since there was a community centre there. Cuts and austerity measures have left this town and the rest of the region struggling to provide facilities for those who need them most.' I smiled at him. 'They may even have things for senior citizens. We can pop over and have a look once we finish here.'

He peered at me and then at the crowd outside the community centre.

'I might meet a young woman.'

I laughed. 'Well, maybe one not so young.'

'They have plenty on offer for old duffers like you, Frank,' Lydia said.

'What do you mean?'

She showed me her mobile. 'According to their website, the community centre runs several classes for the over 40s, including cross-stitch, line dancing, and a book club.' She smirked at me. 'Can you even read, Frank?'

I grabbed the phone from her. 'I didn't know that Eva Cross was cutting the ribbon for the official ceremony.'

Lydia sipped at her drink. 'Is she another of your old girlfriends?'

'What do you mean about old girlfriends?'

'Jack's told me all about your dalliances with the barmaid from the Fat Ox.' She narrowed her eyes at me. 'Or did I get it wrong and you've been stepping out with a fat ox?'

I finished my pint. 'I've had a few dates with Judy, but that's it. Nothing is going on between us.'

Lydia waved her empty glass at me. 'So there is still hope for the good doctor, Kitty Carlisle?' She looked at my father. 'Did you hear that, Jack? Your favourite son wants to marry a doctor.'

He peered at me. 'Good. Then they can help me with my bunions.'

'How do you know Dr Carlisle's first name?' I said.

Lydia removed a bit of fish from her teeth. 'Jack told me.'

My old man cradled the glass in his wrinkled hands.

'Have you been talking to Dr Carlisle about me, Dad?'

Cider glistened on his lips. 'I think she fancies you.'

'Do people still use that phrase?'

Lydia grinned. 'No online dating for you, Frank?'

I grimaced at the thought. 'Meeting people online is never a good thing.'

She put one hand on her heart. 'Oh, you poor thing, you don't know what you're missing. You could wow people with your charmament.'

'Charmament?'

'You're still living in the romantic dark ages, Walker. Charmament is an arsenal of weapons of seduction.' She looked me up and down. 'Though I'm struggling to see what they are at the moment. You're just a saddict.'

'Okay, now I know you're making these words up.'

She shook her head. 'Nope, it's a legitimate term. A saddict is somebody who thrives on misery.'

My father lifted a shaky hand and pointed at the community centre. 'Are we going there?'

I stood and grabbed the handles of the wheelchair.

'Yes, we might as well make a day out of it.'

Lydia joined us as we crossed the road, all three of us smelling of cider and fish and chips, as I tried not to think about Dr Kitty Carlisle.

3 CLOUDBUSTING

The clouds darkened as the air fizzed with electricity. I glanced at the gulls as they ate discarded chips, the taste of vinegar still in my throat as the smell of saltwater lingered everywhere.

'Who's Eva Cross?' Lydia said as we approached the community centre.

I tightened my grip on the wheelchair to ensure no accidents. I'd taken the old man out last week and forgot to fasten the seat belt around him. That nearly ended in disaster when I hit a kerb on the way to the park. He was halfway to cracking his head on the concrete when I pulled him up.

'She's the wealthy woman who funded the building and staffing of the community centre.'

Lydia shook her head. 'I should have guessed it wasn't the government doing this.' We were close to the entrance. 'Is Cross local?'

I stopped to straighten my father's shirt and clean the bits of chips off the collar. He picked something from his teeth and flicked it against the wall.

'She was thirty years ago. Then she went to Australia, where she married a rich man and turned his money into a successful property business. He died last year and now she's here spending her cash on good causes.'

Lydia peered at me. 'Are you Facebook friends with her? Is she another former squeeze?'

I laughed at her. 'Squeeze? Do people still use that word?'

I expected her to teach me another lesson in modern dating, but she didn't.

'Don't deflect from the questions, Walker.'

'No, I'm not her friend on any social media platform, though that's where I got all that information from.'

'But you are the same age?'

I thought about it. 'Similar, I guess.' I looked at the building. 'I'm from Whiteport, not Billsdale, so I never visited the old community centre on this spot, but I suppose Cross must have since she's from the town.'

Spots of rain drizzled out of the sky.

'Did you come here as a kid, visiting the seaside and making sandcastles?'

I glanced at the old man snoring in his seat.

'Rarely. I went to a few gigs in the early 90s at the Billsdale Bowl, but they and it are long-distance memories now.'

I'd forgotten both the good and bad that happened around here then. The most prominent memories were of my first gig at the Bowl, seeing Kirsty MacColl when I was sixteen. It wasn't so much the music I remembered but the group of older teenagers who tried to steal my watch. A punch to the guts soon deterred them from such a foolish idea, and they spent the rest of the night avoiding me.

Lydia stared at me in amazement. 'It's hard to believe

you were once a carefree teenager enjoying the pleasures of live music, booze and girls.'

I peered over her shoulder at the sea, watching the waves crash into the offshore wind turbines. Those windmills weren't there when I was a kid. They looked like giants coming to smash the town to pieces.

'I've still got a bit of life in me.'

She nodded beyond me. 'Unlike some of them in there.'

I followed her gaze, staring at the group of people surrounding Eva Cross.

'Don't you recognise the northeast's former celebrities, Lydia?'

She shook her head. 'Should I? I've lived in Whiteport all my life and don't know any of them.'

'That's probably because they're not from your generation, but mine and Eva's.' I pointed at the large man with a shock of curly hair. 'That's Jim Furman. He was a teenage footballing wonder kid for Whiteport. He only played a few games in the first team before Manchester United signed him up to join their bunch of promising youngsters, including David Beckham.' She frowned at me. 'You must have heard of him.'

'He has nice hair and even better tattoos,' she said. 'Did Furman become a superstar?'

'Unfortunately not. He suffered an injury not long after moving to Manchester. I don't know what happened to him after that.' We moved closer to the group. 'The bald bloke talking to Furman is Paul Lawrence. He opened his own clothes shop here and eventually took his business to a bigger, better store in London. He was the darling of the fashion world for most of the '90s. I may even have bought one of his suits when I worked at the Met.' Lydia narrowed her eyes at me. 'The woman next to him is Julia Jones, a former supermodel. The guy who looks like Mick Jagger is Pete Blom, a singer-songwriter.'

'Never heard of him,' she said.

'He's not a frontman anymore, writing songs for others or playing in other people's bands. I think he might have replaced Phil Collins on drums for Genesis once. I don't know who the rest of the group are.'

'But they're all local?'

'At one time. Then they upped sticks for pastures new.'

She smiled at me. 'Just like you.'

'Yeah, I guess so. And we've all ended up back here.'

Lydia touched my arm. 'I assume they'll all leave once they finish their business here, but what about you, Frank?' She glanced at my slumbering father and I knew what she meant. 'How long are you hanging around for?'

'I haven't made any decisions yet.'

'Jesus Christ, Frank Walker.'

A tall bloke built for professional wrestling strode towards me.

'He's one, but not the other,' Lydia said. 'Though I'm sure he has a cult of followers living in a basement somewhere.'

I glared at her as the man held out a hand to me. 'We went to school together, Frank.' I peered into his brown eyes, distracted by the scar on his cheek and how his shoulder-length hair smelt of strawberries. 'Dennis Garbutt, remember?'

His handshake was firm enough to squeeze my bones, but I had no recollection of this man from my youth.

Lydia nodded at him. 'I know you – you wrote that book about serial killers.'

Garbutt's teeth were perfectly white as he beamed at her.

'*A British History of Serial Killers.* It was an Amazon Top Seller for weeks.'

I still had no recollection of him. 'You're here for the centre opening?'

'I am, Frank. Would you like a signed copy of the book?' I didn't reply. 'Maybe we can spend some time together later, so I can ask about Christopher Matthews.'

'Perhaps,' I said as I gripped onto the wheelchair. 'I need to get my dad inside now.'

I turned from Garbutt as Lydia leaned into me.

'You can make some money from talking to him, Walker.'

'The last thing I want is to speak about Matthews again.'

Matthews was the serial killer I'd helped put away but had lost my job because of it.

As music blared out of the speakers, we moved further into the building.

She nodded her head. 'I've heard this before. What is it?'

'*Something Good* by Utah Saints,' I said.

She whistled a few bars of the tune. 'Where do I know that female vocal from?'

'It's a sample from Kate Bush's *Cloudbusting.*'

The noise woke the old man. 'The bombs are dropping. We've got to get to the shelter.' Panic possessed his eyes as his lips quivered.

I knelt in front of him. 'It's only music, Dad. There are no bombs.'

His eyes watered as he peered at me. 'You call that music? That's not music. Bing Crosby and Vera Lynn, that's music.'

'You sound just like my dad.' Eva Cross had left her admirers to join us. 'I bet you like Glenn Miller as well.'

The old man's face lit up like a UFO over a nuclear power station.

'You got that right, young lady.' He leant forward in the wheelchair with only the belt stopping him from falling out and grabbing her. 'Are you Frank's wife? He never brings you to see me.'

Cross's smile glistened, her long blonde hair floating behind her like the subject of a Pre-Raphaelite painting. As she moved closer, I smelt the freshness of her perfume and suddenly realised that Lydia was right – I looked like a tramp. And God knows what aromas were coming from me – probably sweat mixed in with fish and chips.

She took my father's hand. 'No, I'm not married, young man.' She looked at me. 'Is Frank your son?'

'One of them,' he said. 'Not the one in prison, the one who used to be a copper until they sacked him.'

The hairs on the back of my neck prickled. 'I resigned, Dad.'

Eva Cross let go of him and turned to me. 'I'm sure you had good reason, Mr...?'

I held my hand to her, forgetting that my fingers were still greasy from the food.

'Walker, but call me Frank.'

She shook my hand. 'Nice to meet you, Frank. Thank you for coming to the grand opening.' She looked at Lydia. 'And is this your daughter?'

Lydia put a hand on her chest as she coughed.

'Please, lady, do you think I look anything like him?'

'Well,' Cross glanced between us, 'I didn't mean to upset anybody, but....'

I could guess what she was thinking.

'Lydia is my friend, Mrs Cross, one too young to know the history of this spot and the people you've gathered to open the new community centre. So I explained it to her, doing my best for local history.'

Lydia must have finally realised what had been going through Cross's mind.

'Wait, you thought Frank and I were...' she grabbed her throat. 'Oh, that's gross.'

Nervous laughter drifted out of Cross before she turned to me.

'Are you from the same era as me, Frank?'

I nodded. 'Born in 1977. Too young for punk but just right for the indie-dance-rave scene of the late 80s and early 90s.' I smiled at Lydia. 'I was just telling my young friend how I used to go to gigs not far from here.'

Step On by the Happy Mondays bounced into the air as I spoke. It was a great song, but it was a strange choice for the occasion until I glanced around and saw people my age and older bopping their heads to the tune.

Eva Cross beamed at me. 'Perhaps I should ask them to play *God's Cop* instead?'

I snorted at the thought of it. 'Probably not, considering the lyrics aren't very flattering.'

'Spin some Kate Bush,' Lydia said. 'She's all the rage with the kids right now.'

'Stranger things have happened,' I said.

Cross didn't appear to get my little joke. 'Still, most people here seem to be enjoying the music.'

I looked across the room and saw she was right. Even my father was tapping his fingers on the arm of the wheelchair.

'Those older folks at the back don't like it by the grumpy looks on their faces.'

'Ah, yes,' Eva Cross said. 'They're some of the last remaining staff from the original community centre. Most of them are in their seventies, so I guess indie-dance-rave isn't really their thing.' She looked at my father. 'Though your dad appears to be enjoying himself.'

He did as well. Perhaps the sun, sea air and the cider had done him some good.

'Will you be returning to Australia when this is over?' I said to her, hoping the disappointment in my voice wasn't as apparent to her as it was to me.

She pursed her lips. 'I'm not sure, Frank. I've got some other business to conclude before deciding my future.'

Lydia shivered in her oversized jumper. 'Why would you live in this terrible climate when you can have the sun all year round?'

Eva scrutinised the younger woman. 'Well, there is something to be said about living in an environment that changes over the seasons and appreciating all that nature offers. And I miss the snow sometimes.'

Lydia shrugged. 'You can take it with you. Give me sunshine any day of the week.'

Eva reached out and touched my arm, a movement that made my legs tremble, and I wished once more that I'd worn trousers instead of shorts.

'Tonight, there's a reception here for the official opening of the building. So why don't the three of you come along as my guests?'

I wanted to accept immediately, but had enough willpower to resist for at least twenty seconds. Then Lydia got in before me.

'Definitely, as long as Frank smartens himself up. I'm not going out with him again looking like that.'

'I have a suit,' I said.

She shook her head. 'Is it in mothballs?'

Eva Cross laughed. 'There's no dress code here – you can wear what you want.'

Lydia glared at me. 'You need to shower, shave, brush your teeth, and wear something at least half-decent. And I'll find a fragrance to spray you with.'

I suddenly felt self-conscious about how I smelt and looked.

'That's settled then,' Eva said. 'Come back here at eight tonight.'

She left us to join the others as the music changed to *Insane in the Brain* by Cypress Hill. As I turned to the old man, a thousand bees buzzed inside my skull.

'Did you hear that, Dad? You're going to a fancy party.'

He was still tapping his fingers as I went to him, seeing the vacant stare in his eyes and realising he hadn't been with us for a while.

4 SISTER MORPHINE

The old man's face glazed over as I wiped the drool from his lips.

'Is he okay?' Lydia said.

My heart was sinking into my feet. 'It's one of his fugue states. He hasn't had one for a while but normally snaps out of them after a few minutes.'

I peered into the whiteness of his eyes as a bunch of kids bounced up and down on a giant trampoline across the road. His fingers were icy in mine, the wrinkles of his skin rubbing against the scars on my palm. He looked as if he was preparing for the next world and I tore my hand and gaze from him. I glanced behind me, staring into the community centre, to see Eva Cross mingling with her guests, watching as the famous ex-residents of this sleepy seaside town signed autographs and posed for selfies with an admiring crowd.

My father's breathing was slow and laboured, drawing my focus back to him and away from the local celebrities. They were hardly at the pinnacle of fame, but they'd be remembered long after me and the old man were gone.

Who would remember us? I doubted my sisters thought much about me, never mind their father. I was unsure I'd tell them about his passing after he was gone. I suppose I would have to, but it would be bad enough visiting my brother in prison to inform him. I'd had no contact with my sisters for years, but I knew they were both on social media, so I could message them through Facebook.

Hi Mary, Hi Colleen. It's your long-lost brother Frank; just getting in touch to let you know the old man has died.

That thought was the final push to knock the stuffing right out of me. Then Lydia grabbed my hand.

'We have to do something, Frank. He's not moving.'

My knees creaked as I bent to peer into my father's face. The mist had cleared from his eyes, but nothing was behind them. I took his wrist with trepidation, feeling for a pulse.

It was there, faint but moving against my finger. I pushed the growing anxiety in my chest deep into my gut, releasing his hand as I stood.

'We need to call an ambulance and get him to the hospital.'

'That'll take too long,' Lydia said. 'We'll go in my car.'

I nodded and grabbed the wheelchair, pushing it as Lydia went to where she'd parked. She opened the back door and helped me get him inside. He was so light I probably could have done it without her, but I noticed she was as concerned about him as I was.

Picking him up was like lifting an empty set of clothes, the bones in his legs pressing against my hands. His lips were moving, but his voice was so low it was impossible to hear his words.

At least he was alive.

For now.

I strapped him into the back and got into the passenger

seat. Lydia didn't say anything as she drove off, and we settled into a stony silence during the twenty-minute journey to the hospital. She parked outside the front of the building, next to the entrance for Accident and Emergency.

'Can you find Dr Carlisle while I get him out?' I said to her. She agreed without speaking, jumping out of the car as I removed the wheelchair from the boot. Then I strapped him in and pushed the chair into the hospital.

Chaos greeted us. Over a dozen adults were standing in the middle of the room, with upturned chairs scattered around them. The noise level was louder than the worst heavy metal disco, a combination of screaming, crying and angry howls. Two nurses were trying to deal with the cacophony, one tall, the other small, their expressions as anguished as the surrounding faces. I looked for Lydia, unable to find her as I saw the security guards moving towards the agitated crowd.

'A car drove into a bunch of folks in the town centre.' I turned to see Lydia next to me. 'Four people have serious injuries.'

'Terrorists,' the voice below me said.

Relief swept through me as I dropped to his level.

'Are you okay, Dad?'

Life had returned to his eyes and face. His lips trembled as he spoke.

'I am now we got away from those terrorists.'

Lydia touched his hand. 'It wasn't terrorists, Jack.' She glanced at me. 'A drunk driver came off the road onto the pavement.'

She was trying to minimise the shock for his sake, but I knew it would be impossible after looking at the nurses and security talking to the distressed group.

'Did you find Dr Carlisle?'

Lydia nodded. 'She's on her way.' One of the crying women collapsed to the floor. 'Perhaps we should move away from this.'

I agreed, pushing my father out of A&E and into the corridor. I tried to ignore the noise and spoke to the old man again.

'Are you sure you're okay, Dad?'

His eyes were wide and bright, looking as alive as I'd seen him in a long time.

'I need a drink, Frank. Is there a pub nearby?'

I laughed and sat beside him, letting the smile warm my face.

'I think we could all do with one.'

Lydia slumped next to me. 'You got that right, but I'm driving, so it will have to wait until we get back.'

I didn't argue with her, staring at my father and wondering how much more of this I could take. How much more of it could he take? Dr Kitty Carlisle appeared as I struggled for an answer.

'Hello, Jack. I hear you haven't been feeling too well.'

He grinned at her. 'It's nothing a pint of cider won't cure.'

Dr Carlisle bent to get close to his face, peering hard into his eyes. Then she took his hand and checked the old man's pulse.

'I'd like to move you upstairs for a few tests first, Jack. Is that all right with you?'

What remained of his teeth sparkled as he smiled at her. 'You can take me anywhere.'

She returned his smile as she let go of him and stood, turning to me.

'Is that all right with you, Frank?'

A mixture of relief and nervous tension surrounded my heart.

'Of course, Dr Carlisle. Can we come with you?'

She nodded. 'Follow me.'

So we did, with me pushing the old man down the corridor and into a lift. We stepped out of it two floors up, and Kitty called a nurse to take my father into a private room.

'This shouldn't be long,' she said as she closed the door on us.

Lydia pulled me into a seat after I stood there like a confused statue.

'I'm sure he'll be fine, Frank.'

A poster on the wall urged people to wash their hands.

'I don't think he has many fine days left, Lydia.'

We sat in silence as I pushed all the worrying thoughts about my father deep into the dark corners of my head. Instead, I pictured those we'd seen in A&E, considering how quickly one person's actions could change the lives of those they'd never met.

I'd returned to the family home after quitting the police, not with any great desire to reconnect with my father, but because I had nowhere else to go. Then I convinced myself I was only staying to look after the old man, even though he'd shown no interest in me as a child or teenager. It was the same with my older brother Tommy, so I assumed my father had been as indifferent to my sisters as he was with us. So I wasn't sure why I was still living with him.

Was I only waiting for him to die before leaving again?

I thought about my errant siblings: two older sisters who'd abandoned the family home at their first opportunity and a brother currently looking at the world through prison bars.

What did I owe them?

Nothing.

What did I owe the old man?

There was a debt to pay, but it wasn't to him: it was to me. A promise to be the best person I could be, no matter how difficult I might find it. And that meant sticking with my father regardless of my suppressed feelings towards him.

'Jack's fine.'

I looked up to see Kitty Carlisle standing over me. I took a deep breath before speaking.

'Was it another of his fugue states?'

'It seems likely, Frank.' She clutched a bunch of papers in her arms. 'But I'd like to keep him in overnight to be on the safe side. What do you think?'

I wanted to stop thinking, go to the pub with Lydia and drink until the only thing inside my head was a warm fuzziness that obliterated everything else.

However, I didn't tell her that.

'I bow down to your expertise.' I smiled at her. 'Should I return in the morning?'

She returned my smile, radiating warmth that made my legs giddy.

'I'll ring you first.'

I stood and shook her hand, enjoying the touch of her skin against mine.

'I look forward to it.'

Lydia grimaced, and I knew the words had come out all wrong as soon as I said them. But Kitty didn't seem to mind, smiling at me as she returned to her work. All I could do was stand there with my mouth half-open until Lydia dragged me away.

She bundled me into the lift. 'You need to put your tongue away, Frank.'

I licked the top of my lips and frowned at her. 'I don't know what you're on about.'

The lift descended as I leaned into the poster warning about sexually transmitted diseases.

'You know all right, Mr Walker. The glint in your eyes speaks volumes.'

I let Lydia have her fun, understanding she was only doing it to take my mind off what had happened to the old man.

At least, I thought that's what she was doing.

'You think I'm drooling over Dr Carlisle while my father is ill?'

'You look like a frog every time you see her, Frank, all bulging eyes and sweaty forehead.'

I touched the top of my head and grimaced. 'You thought I was interested in Eva Cross a few hours ago.'

She shrugged. 'Who's to say you can't fancy two people simultaneously?'

We stepped out of the lift and went past A&E, which had calmed down from earlier. An angry security guard was waiting outside, pointing at Lydia's car and glaring at us. I left her to work her charm on him and slipped into the back seat. It didn't take her long.

'Shall I drop you home for a nap before tonight?' she said.

'Tonight?'

'Eva Cross's party at the new community centre. I'm assuming you still want to go.'

Did I?

'Do you?'

She grinned as she drove out of the hospital grounds and onto the main road.

'Sure, why not? I've got nothing better to do. Have you?'

'An empty house, four cans of cider and the movie version of *Doctor Sleep*.'

Lydia turned up her nose. 'Meh. It's okay, but the book's far superior. I hate that they changed the ending.'

'The book is always better than the film. So you think we should still go to this soirée?'

'Of course. It might give us the chance to take our minds off other things.'

She was right, but I wasn't sure it would work. So I got Lydia to drop me off at home – the old man's home, never mine – but there was no nap on the agenda. I told her to pick me up at seven-thirty and then went into the empty house.

As I stepped inside, the ghosts were already waiting for me.

5 TAKE ME OUT

Lydia was dead on time. She whistled loudly as I stepped out of the house, wearing an ice blue suit and a new short haircut.

'So, you can try when you want to,' she said.

I got into the car, scrutinising her outfit: a vibrant purple ensemble of jacket and trousers that matched her hair colour.

'You're no wallflower yourself.'

'There's no point in going to a party unless you're prepared to make an impression.' She drove away from the house. 'But I guess you never enjoyed yourself in London.'

I turned the radio to 6 Music, listening to Self Esteem.

'I'll have you know I was a regular gig-goer in the capital, enjoying myself as much as anybody your age.'

She grinned at me. 'Are you going to tell me about your sordid social life on the way to the community centre?'

'Don't be so cheeky. There was nothing sordid about it.'

'So, no tales of sex, drugs, and rock and roll? That's such a disappointment.'

Lydia laughed, and I joined her. I knew she was still

trying to distract me from thoughts of the old man in the hospital, and I was glad of that.

'Maybe I'll tell you all about it when you're older.'

Her laugh disappeared, and she narrowed her eyes at me.

'How old do you think I am, Frank?'

I peered at Lydia's purple suit, picturing her the first time we met six months ago, when she looked like a teenage goth.

'Eighteen?'

She shook her head. 'Are you using the observational skills you picked up in the Metropolitan Police?'

A sudden terrible thought struck me. She looked older than eighteen, but maybe she was younger.

'Are you old enough to drink alcohol?' I'd bought her booze on more than one occasion.

'Don't worry, Frank – you haven't broken any laws.' The music changed to Goldfrapp singing about a *Strict Machine*. 'Not with me, anyway.'

'Well, I don't know about you, Lydia, but I'll be downing a few tonight.'

'You and me both, Mr Walker. Soon as I park the car near my flat, it's only a short walk to the community centre. And I'll keep a close eye on you at this shindig.'

I pulled at the tie choking my neck. 'Why? To make sure I don't drink too much?'

'Oh no – you can drink as much as you want. In fact, I encourage it.'

'So why will you be watching me?'

'You know why, Frank.' She pointed at my suit. 'You're dressed for some romancing tonight, aren't you?'

'Romancing? Who with?'

Lydia pulled onto the main Billsdale road, so we were only a few minutes from her place.

'Isn't it obvious?'

'Not to me,' I said.

She switched off the radio as we approached her flat.

'Eva Cross, of course.'

I was lost for words as she parked the car. I still hadn't found them as we got out, and she locked the vehicle.

'Do you need the toilet before we head over, Frank?'

The suit was tight around my waist – the only other time I'd worn it was my last day with the Met – as I twisted my face to her, catching the end of the evening sun.

'I'm fine, Lydia. What about you?'

She reached into her handbag and removed some lipstick, adding an extra shine of purple to her lips before returning it to the bag and putting that over her shoulder.

'No. Let's get to this party and hope they have some champagne.'

We strode down the road, past flickering amusement arcades, most of which were empty of paying customers. I glanced beyond the sea wall, peering at the shimmering orange sinking below the horizon. Since leaving the car, the wind had risen, drawing the waves against the turbines gazing over the town. Even into my mid-forties, I pictured them as a child might, seeing giants standing in the water, not knowing if they were there to protect us or were waiting to invade.

Lydia reached the entrance, pushing the door open and turning to me.

'The first drink is on you, Walker.'

I followed her inside. 'I'm still not convinced you're of legal age for alcohol, Lydia Thompson.'

She waved a hand at me before moving towards a crowd

of people. I left her to it, scrutinising the surroundings more than I had in the afternoon. A prominent notice board with the heading *Welcome to the NEW Billsdale Community Centre* was to my right. There was space underneath it for a display, but it was empty. I went to it and touched the surface, running my fingers over the cork. Small bits of it came away on my skin.

'Your hands are rougher than they look.'

I turned to see Eva Cross next to me. Her eyes were bluer than the sea, her complexion as perfect as new porcelain. She wore a dark dress that clung to her body.

I looked at my palm as I smiled at her. 'It runs in the family.'

She reached over and touched my shoulder. 'I heard about your father – I'm sorry, Frank.'

How did she know about that?

I touched her fingers. 'Thank you.'

She didn't remove my hand. 'I'm glad you came tonight. I hope we can ease some of your anxiety.'

Eva must have felt my fingers trembling, but she misunderstood why.

'I hope so, as well.' I glanced behind her at the empty board. 'Are you missing something on the display?'

She finally moved her hand from mine. 'My staff are looking for photos from the original community centre so we can have a timeline from then to now.'

'I got you a drink, Walker.' Lydia joined us, handing me a glass of champagne. 'Sorry, Eva, but I didn't get you one.'

Eva waved away the apology. 'Don't worry about it. I haven't touched alcohol in twenty years.'

I guessed why she was tea-total from the look in her eyes, but Lydia barged in with the personal question.

'Why's that, Eva?'

Eva's lips glistened as she spoke. 'My father was a violent alcoholic, and the memories keep me from touching a drop. But don't let my sobriety stop you.'

Lydia raised her glass. 'Don't worry; it won't.'

Eva slipped her arm into mine. 'Come, there's food waiting for us.'

She led me towards the main hall, my mind a confusing mix of delight at the smell of her jasmine perfume and sorrow at what she'd said about her father. I decided not to pursue that subject as we joined the others, and Lydia headed straight for the refreshments. She pushed past a group circulating among the local celebs, ignoring the frowns of a bunch of women as the former professional footballer Jim Furman turned his attention from them to Lydia. He was my age, and I transformed into a concerned parent as I watched him lick his lips as Lydia downed her champagne.

'I wish I'd known about his difficulties before inviting Furman to this gathering,' Eva said.

I sipped on my drink as I faced her. 'You mean the accident that ended his football career?'

Eva shook her head. 'No, it was what happened after that.'

She didn't expand upon that, but I guessed what she meant as I watched Furman down a glass of champagne and snatch another from a startled serving girl. I'd seen enough functioning alcoholics at the Met to recognise one when they were on their best behaviour. Two women dragged him away from the food table, so at least he wasn't leering at Lydia.

'I guess you had to scrape the bottom of the barrel when looking for local celebs to open this place.'

'Oh, I don't know,' Eva said. 'Blom might not be in the

charts anymore, but he's still successful in what he does. And Julia Jones is one of those supermodels who never go out of fashion, no matter how old she is.'

I glanced at Jones, her emerald eyes mesmerising me from fifty feet away. She was taller than me, over six feet, but that could have been because of her giant high heels. Her long dress matched the colour of her eyes, finished off with a dark cloak, making her appear like a sophisticated vampire.

Ice slipped down my throat as I spoke. 'I hope I look that good when I'm fifty.'

Eva curled her lips and laughed at me. 'You sound like a fan.'

'Not really. I remember her being all over the magazine covers when I arrived in London in 1995.'

'Is that so? I seem to recall gazing at glossy photos of Brad Pitt and David Duchovny in 1995.'

The glint in her eyes made my heart skip a beat.

'Well, Eva, the truth is out there.'

Two young women approached us, but Eva dragged me in the other direction.

'The twins have been pestering me since I got off the plane in Newcastle.'

I enjoyed her grip on my arm again. 'Twins?'

She led me into another room filled with books, children's toys, and games.

'Cynthia and Alison Holgate. They were the ones who contacted me in Australia about this project to build a new community centre in Billsdale. And, don't get me wrong, I was happy to do it, but they never stop rabbiting on whenever they're near me.'

I glanced over my shoulder to see the disappointed faces

of the twins. They returned to the others as we stopped at a table covered in books.

'Well, you've accomplished a grand job with the building. I'm sure it will be a big hit with the locals.'

She let go of me and picked up a tattered paperback of Mario Puzo's *The Godfather*.

'Oh, I haven't done much but provide the funding. The twins and a core of volunteers completed all the hard work of acquiring the land, talking to the builders, and then recruiting staff.' Eva put the book back. 'So I shouldn't be so hard on them, but sometimes you need a break from other people.' She peered into my eyes. 'Do you understand what I mean?'

I did – more than she'd ever realise.

'Of course, Eva. So say when you've had enough of me.'

Her laugh was the sound of an angel getting its wings.

'We've only just met, Frank. I haven't got to know you yet.'

'That's what I'm worried about.'

She dragged me from the books to the large stack of board games in the corner. I focused on the cover of *Dungeons and Dragons*, peering at a flaming purple dragon as it swooped towards a castle, thinking about Lydia and her outfit.

Eva squeezed my arm. 'Tell me what it was like arriving in London for the first time in 1995.'

The purple dragon glared at me. '1995 wasn't my first time in the capital. Three years earlier, I'd hitchhiked down with a group of mates to see Prince at Earl's Court. That's when I knew I'd live and work there one day.'

'Prince? Wow! That must have been impressive.'

'To be honest, I can't remember much about it. The passage of time is no great friend to the human brain.' Her eyes fixed on mine. 'I dare say my life in London wasn't as exciting as yours in Australia.'

The light disappeared from her face, replaced with darkness I was all too familiar with: somebody dealing with grief.

'Things were as good as they'd ever been in my life until, well... I assume you know what happened.'

'I'm sorry about your husband's passing, Eva.'

She twisted her head to peer at the empty ceiling, releasing an inaudible sigh as she returned to me.

'Thankfully, it was a brief illness.' She scrutinised the contents of the room. 'And the twins have given me something to focus my mind on.'

I didn't know what to say, so I blurted out the thing I hadn't spoken to anybody about.

'My wife left me.'

'Oh,' she said.

I felt like a fool for saying it, unsure what to do next. My phone ringing saved me from that. I smiled at Eva as I removed the mobile and answered it.

'Are you checking up on me, Sara?'

Detective Inspector Sara Rose – the only other friend apart from Lydia I'd made on my return home.

'You need to meet me at the mortuary, Frank.'

The mortuary? My legs shook as I placed my free hand on the table of books.

'Is it...?'

I couldn't mention the old man's name.

'It's a murder investigation, Frank.'

'Murder? Is this about Tommy?'

Tommy, my older brother, the convicted killer.

'I'm unsure what it is. That's why I need you to meet me at the mortuary.'

Once I knew it wasn't about my father, my legs stabilised.

'I'm not a copper anymore, Sara.'

'We've discovered your name at the crime scene, Frank.'

I laughed aloud. 'There are plenty of Frank Walker's in the world, Sara. There's even a popular Canadian musician called that.'

She sighed down the line. 'I don't think it was his name we found stuffed inside the victim's stomach.'

My guts rumbled as she hung up on me.

I was off to the mortuary, and I still hadn't eaten.

Lydia drove me to the mortuary. I didn't ask her how much she'd drank at the community centre in our short visit, but she looked sober. She parked outside the same hospital containing my father.

'That community centre is jinxed already,' she said.

I undid the seatbelt in no rush to get to the room of the dead.

'What do you mean?'

She turned to me. 'Well, the first time we visited, your dad had his fugue, and we ended up here. And now, after our second trip there, we're back at the hospital with you going to the mortuary to find out why a murder victim has your name inside their body.'

I peered through the windscreen at the entrance, a different one from where we'd stepped into A&E earlier in the day.

'The Rose Cottage or Rainbow's End – which do you prefer?'

Concern filled her face. 'Are you okay, Frank?'

I removed a piece of dirt from the leg of my sparkling blue suit.

'In my earliest days as a police officer, I visited a hospital to speak to parents who were unaware their teenage daughter had died. They were looking at me expectantly when we heard the voice over the tannoy: *"Can a porter please go to bed ten on Ward B. Sophia Gordon needs taking to Rose Cottage, thank you."*'

Lydia guessed what it meant. 'They used Rose Cottage as a euphemism for the mortuary?'

I nodded. 'Rose Cottage and Rainbow's End are sometimes used in British hospitals to enable discussions about death in front of patients. They were adopted so announcements concerning the mortuary could be made without upsetting anyone.'

'How many grieving family members and friends did you speak to as a copper?'

'Far too many.' I got out of the car. 'You don't have to wait for me, Lydia.'

This time, she was in a proper parking space. 'I'm not going anywhere, Frank.'

She switched the radio on, so I heard Lou Reed singing about a perfect day as I entered. I followed the signs to the mortuary, finding it at the end of the hospital complex.

I rang the bell and waited.

Two minutes later, a tall man wearing green scrubs opened the door. I thought I'd stepped into a movie production for one second because he was the spitting image of the actor Idris Elba. He removed surgical gloves and dropped them into his pockets.

'Can I help you?' he said.

I peered at his name badge. 'I'm looking for DI Sara Rose, Dr Patterson.'

He wiped the sweat from his forehead. 'Ah, you must be Mr Walker.'

'That's right.'

'Okay. Follow me.'

I went down a long corridor, through a set of swing doors, and into a large room. I'd been inside mortuaries numerous times before, but the sights and aromas always hit you the same way, a reminder that time was fleeting. Several gurneys contained bodies wrapped in white plastic, while the smell of strong disinfectant lay over everything.

When you first see a dead body, you cannot prepare for it no matter what people tell you beforehand about what to expect. You're looking at someone who was alive not long before, a loved one that would be mourned and missed. I'd known people over the years – fellow officers, medical staff – who'd had to grow indifferent to death to save their sanity.

But I could never do that, and even then, staring at those gurneys, I wished I was anywhere else.

'Are you a pathologist, Dr Patterson?'

He stopped walking and turned to me.

'I am, Mr Walker. If you were looking to speak to the coroner, she's not here.'

I gazed beyond him at the bodies wrapped in plastic, waiting for them to jump out as if in some terrible horror film.

'I don't want to speak to anybody here, Dr Robertson – no offence.'

'It's too late for that, Frank.' DI Sara Rose stepped out of the shadows like a ghost appearing at a cemetery. She nodded at Robertson and grabbed me. She dragged me from the doctor and the bodies, returning to the corridor. 'You were supposed to wait for me outside.'

Her arm in mine wasn't as pleasant as Eva's earlier.

'I must have missed that part of the message.'

She hauled me into a room with Dr Robertson's name on the door. Sara sat in the leather chair opposite a desk containing a computer and family photos. I glanced at the certificates displaying the pathologist's expertise.

'Sit down, Frank. We might be a while.'

I resisted the urge to leave and did as instructed.

'You know I like it when you take charge, DI Rose.'

'Do you know David Cash?'

I thought about it before shaking my head. 'Should I?'

She removed a mobile phone from her jacket and threw it at me. I did my best cricket impersonation and caught it one-handed.

'Touch the screen and examine the photos.'

I flicked my finger across the device and went through the images: a plastic bag covered in blood; the same bag opened with a piece of paper removed from it; the paper with my name on it. And it was stained red.

'And you found this inside David Cash's stomach?'

'We did. Are you sure you don't know him?'

I shrugged. 'Nope. I guess I could have met him some time. Who was he?'

Sara peered deep into my eyes. 'He was a seventy-five-year-old retired journalist, murdered tonight in the home where he'd lived for fifty years. Could he have written something about you at some point?'

'I don't know. Is he from London?'

'No. He lived in Billsdale all his life. His wife died six years ago, and there were no children or other family. So why did we find your name on a piece of paper inside his guts?'

I couldn't answer the question. 'How did it get there?'

'We're guessing whoever killed him made him eat it during the torture.'

A shiver ran down my spine. 'Torture?'

'At least several hours of it. Do you want to see the crime scene photos?'

I didn't, but I knew I'd have to. I glanced again at the qualifications on the wall.

'Sure.'

She pointed at the phone in my hand. 'Keep going on there.'

The next photo showed a smiling grey-haired old man with a wrinkled face and fading blue eyes. I didn't recognise him and said so. She told me to continue with the photos.

The second image was of a living room. Even through the pixels, it was easy to spot the blood staining the carpet. A memory of my time in the Met and visiting dozens of violent crime scenes clouded my vision. Then I continued, seeing David Cash again, but there was no smile on his face: only pain and death. Blood filled his eyes, and his cheeks were sunk deep into his skull. A terrible sight only got worse when I moved from the close-up to the next photo of the body.

The phone trembled in my hands. 'They crucified him upside down?'

Sara nodded. 'And he's not the first.'

I returned the mobile to her. 'What?'

'We've kept the details from the public and the media, but I'm not sure how long that will continue.' She took a deep breath. 'The first victim was an eighty-year-old farmer, Robert Baker, crucified upside down in his farmhouse two weeks ago. Then, last week, we discovered the second body – Harold Burke, a seventy-seven-year-old retired solicitor.

His wife was away at a writing retreat when it happened. And now we have David Cash.'

'All three of them crucified upside down?'

She clutched her phone. 'Yes. Do you know the other victims?'

My knees creaked as I leaned forward. 'Am I suspect, Sara?'

'No, Frank, but whoever killed Cash forced him to eat a plastic bag containing your name. So you understand I have to speak to you about it and ask if you knew the others.'

'I don't. Did you find my name inside the other victims?'

She shook her head. 'I would have contacted you before if we had.'

'Do you have any clues or suspects?'

'You know I can't tell you those things, Frank.'

I got up to leave. 'I'll be off, then.'

Sara didn't move. 'Sit down, Walker.'

I stared at her. 'So, it's official then?'

'The Chief Constable has made it so regarding you.'

I flopped back into the seat. 'The Chief Constable?'

She nodded. 'The Big Cheese himself. I have to take you to the crime scenes to see if you notice anything.'

'Even if I didn't know the three victims?'

'So says the Cheese.'

I wasn't sure if she was trying to make me laugh or not. Then I remembered the photos, and invisible fingers clawed at my stomach. Perhaps they were looking for a piece of paper with my name on it.

'What if I won't go?'

DI Rose furrowed her eyebrows at me. 'You're refusing to help with a police investigation?'

'I'm not a copper anymore, Sara. So you don't need to

take me to the scenes – just show me the forensic teams' photos and videos.'

'I've never worked a case with you, Frank, but I've spoken to those who have. All your former colleagues speak highly about your work, even those who dislike you, which was most of them. They told me that working a crime scene is a particular skill you possess, having the ability to see things others can't. That's why I need you with me, not just you looking at images.'

'That hasn't convinced me.'

She shook her head. 'I could issue you with an Osman warning.'

'Does that mean Frank gets to be a contestant on *Pointless* or that he'll write a bestselling murder mystery?'

We both turned to see Lydia standing there.

'How did you get past the security?' Rose said.

A mild panic swept through me. 'Is my father okay?'

Lydia touched my arm. 'He's fine. I got bored in the car, so I went to see him. The doctors say he's stable, and there's nothing else we can do for him tonight. So I thought I'd see if you were all right.'

'Is your dad ill?' DI Rose said.

I saw the concern in her eyes. 'He might have had a stroke this afternoon. This is another reason I can't go with you.'

There was sympathy in her face but also steel in her voice.

'You heard Lydia, Frank. Your dad's in the best place for him. It could be good for you to occupy your mind with this while waiting for him to recover.'

Would he recover? And if he did, what state would he be in?

The mortuary odour stuck to the sides of my lungs like glue.

'You think me peering around the scenes of three horrific murders might distract me?'

Lydia spoke before Rose could. 'What's an Osman warning?'

I relaxed at the thought of the old man resting in bed not far from me.

'It's a warning of a death threat or risk of murder, issued by the British police or authorities to a prospective victim. They're used when there is the intelligence of a threat but not enough evidence to justify arresting a potential murderer.' I studied Rose's face. 'Do you think I'm on a serial killer's hit list, Sara?'

She shrugged. 'I'm unsure, Frank. That's why I want you to survey the crime scenes with me, to see if anything jumps out at you.'

'I don't know any of the victims.'

'But the killer knows you – why else would they put your name inside the last victim?'

It was a good question. 'And the post-mortems didn't find my name or anything unusual inside the first two bodies?'

'Not the first time, but I'm having them rechecked. So will you come with me?'

'You know the Osman warning can't force me to go with you.'

'I do, Frank, so I'm appealing to your better nature.'

'He doesn't have one,' Lydia said.

DI Rose faced her with a furrowed brow. 'How did you get in here?'

'Like everybody else, through the door.'

'And where was the security guard?'

Lydia shrugged. 'Probably in the bog.'

I made my decision before they got into a full-scale argument.

'I'll go with you, as long as Lydia comes with me.'

Sara gazed at me through sceptical eyes. 'Why?'

'All the murder scenes are local?'

'Yes,' she said.

'Well, I've only been back here a few months. Lydia knows the area and the people much better than I do. She might be helpful.'

DI Rose puffed out her cheeks and glanced between us.

'Okay, but I don't want you touching anything.' She glared at Lydia. 'And no taking photos or videos.'

Lydia grinned at me. 'Damn. My Twitter and Insta accounts would have gone into overdrive.'

She continued to smile as Sara led us out of the hospital.

7 WRITTEN IN BLOOD

Lydia followed Sara's unmarked police car, into my home town of Whiteport, through its industrial streets, back onto the coast and towards the not-so-sunny seaside spot of Stanport. I remembered my mother taking me there as a kid, wandering through the amusement arcades or strolling on the beach while she went shopping with my Aunt Vi.

Stanport had been a popular coastal resort in the '60s. Still, by the winter of discontent in the '70s and the economic downturn in the '80s, it was on a slippery slope to the faded seaside glamour it had never recovered from.

We turned off the main road and drove through the town centre before arriving on the coast, then travelling beyond the boarded-up shells of the places I visited as a kid. I peered out of the window, remembering those times I spent there, searching out second-hand bookstores and record shops. Somewhere in the old man's house, I still had a collection of battered science fiction paperbacks and scratched seven-inch singles my brother had left behind.

'Somebody swallowed your name?' Lydia said as she kept Sara's car in view.

I nodded. 'Apparently so.'

'And we're going to their house, this person you've never met?'

'David Cash, a former journalist. Do you know the name from the time with your uncle in Whiteport?'

'You mean when Tommy ran his criminal empire with my help?'

'Well, I didn't want to mention that part, but since you did, I'm assuming your uncle or somebody in his organisation would have monitored the local media.'

Sara turned away from the sea into a residential area of properties worthy of the retired middle classes, an endless display of detached bungalows with large, well-kept gardens.

'You're right, Frank. Tommy had several contacts with the local press, but I had nothing to do with them. Even if I did, I doubt there would have been any interaction with a former journalist. How old did you say Cash was?'

'Seventy-five.' Sara pulled up outside a bungalow, and Lydia parked behind her. I turned to my friend. 'You know, I've never been sure what you actually did in Uncle Tommy's criminal organisation.'

She shook her head. 'And you want that conversation now?'

No, I didn't. I removed the seatbelt.

'Of course not.' I grinned at her. 'I'm only messing with you, Lydia.'

We got out, staring at DI Rose waiting for us outside the crime scene. Several police cars and officers were there and suited scenes of crime officers.

Lydia locked the car. 'There's no need for that, Frank. I'm about to get enough trauma inside that bungalow.'

In my urgency to convince Sara to bring Lydia along, I hadn't thought about what it might do to Lydia visiting a murder scene.

'I'm sorry, Lydia, for bringing you here like this. Why don't you wait outside?'

She dismissed my concern with a wave of her hand. 'Let's get on with it.'

'Have you seen a dead body before?'

Lydia turned from the flashing police lights and stared straight into my eyes.

'Didn't Uncle Tommy tell you? I was there when my mother died in the hospital.'

I didn't know what to say; my mouth and brain were frozen in time. Only Sara's voice snapped me out of that haze.

'Are you two coming?'

We moved to her as more SOCOs stepped out of the bungalow. Sara spoke to one of them before turning to us.

'The forensic team have finished inside, so it will only be us now.' She looked at Lydia. 'Are you ready?'

Lydia stuffed her hands into her trouser pockets and I realised how much she stood out in that purple outfit.

'Don't we need to wear protective clothes?'

'If you want,' Sara said. 'But the SOCOs have finished with the crime scene.'

Lydia gazed at the bungalow. 'No, I'm okay. Lead the way, Detective Inspector Rose.'

We followed her inside, stepping past uniformed police officers and into a long narrow corridor. Lydia grimaced and put fingers across her nose, turning to me as the aroma of fresh blood swept over us. As we entered, the smell filled the main room, and Sara nodded at the far wall. Lydia kept a hand on her face, peering at what remained after the SOCOs had removed the victim: the bloodstains surrounding the nails were still dripping into the sodden carpet.

I moved beyond Lydia, closer to the wall, careful where I stood, and thankful the body wasn't there.

'They crucified Cash upside down, Sara?'

She went to show me the photos again, but I stopped her. I didn't need to see them since they were now imprinted in my mind.

'He was, but he suffered before he died.'

'How?' Lydia said.

I didn't want her to hear the graphic details, but Sara continued.

'Once he was nailed to the wall, Cash was flogged. Forensic evidence shows a whip topped with fishhooks was used for the flogging. It ripped the flesh from his stomach, which is how we found the plastic bag with the paper inside.'

'With Walker's name on it?' Lydia said.

Sara nodded.

I continued to stare at the dark red stains. 'Where did you find the skin?'

Sara pointed at the pool of blood on the carpet. 'There, near his head, with the rest of his organs.'

Lydia spoke through her fingers. 'Is that what killed him?'

'No. The killer suspended the victim from his ankles rather than his wrists, so his torso hung downward. The forensic pathologist said Cash's intestines compressed the lungs and diaphragm, so it slowly asphyxiated him. His skull and neck would have been in excruciating pain from the blood's gravitation into the head's blood vessels and from the body's weight driving his head against the ground. Blood pooling in the veins and arteries of the head would probably have kept him conscious for a while. However, the blood would have a harder time getting to the heart and the rest of the body, depriving him of oxygen faster. The coroner will confirm the cause of death after the post-mortem, but the forensic pathologist concluded Cash died from hypovolemic shock when he lost so much blood and fluid his heart couldn't continue to function. But he suffered for hours beforehand.'

Lydia stared at the nails in the wall and the blood-stained carpet before turning and leaving without speaking. I left her and spoke to Sara.

'You said a single killer did this. Are you sure about that?'

She scrutinised me, and I guessed she was thinking about my name inside the victim again.

'You think there was more than one?'

I moved from her, avoiding the blood on the carpet and getting closer to the scene. As well as the four nails forced into the stone, slight marks around each nail made the paint lighter than everywhere else.

'Do you believe one person could have got Cash up against the wall, turned him upside down, and crucified him on their own?'

'No,' she said.

Her eyes fixed on mine, and I knew she wasn't telling me everything. But I wouldn't have expected her to – she was the copper, not me. Not anymore.

I moved away, scanning the rest of the room. 'There were no bloodied footprints?'

She shook her head. 'Whoever did this planned it carefully.'

'As if they'd done the same thing before.'

'They have, Frank – Cash was the third victim crucified upside down.'

'And the killer, or killers, didn't leave anything behind?'

'Only your name inside a plastic bag stuck to the remains of Cash's guts.'

'Did they take bits of Cash with them?'

She shrugged. 'We're not sure yet. The post-mortem will determine that.'

I looked around the rest of the room. 'I've never been here before, Sara, and I don't know who David Cash was.'

'The name doesn't ring any bells?'

'Nope, as I keep telling you.'

'You had no run-ins with journalists when you worked for the Met?'

I was unsure if she was desperate for leads or if this was connected to whatever she was keeping from me.

'There were plenty, Sara, but that was in London and nowhere near here. Are you clutching at straws, or is there something you need to tell me?'

She didn't answer the question. 'Do you want to look through the rest of the house?'

'Do you think the killers spent any time in the other rooms?'

'No.'

'Any witnesses from the neighbours or on the estate?'

'Not so far, but uniformed officers will go door to door. And before you ask, there are no CCTV cameras around here.'

'So, what next, Sara?'

She moved towards the exit. 'We visit the first two crime scenes. As long as you're up for it.'

'Do I have a choice?'

She stepped outside, and I followed, finding Lydia smoking near her car. I frowned at her.

'When did you start that?'

She blew smoke at me. 'Three minutes ago. A neighbour took pity on me.'

I didn't argue with her, knowing I'd only come across as a disgruntled parent again – and I definitely wasn't her father.

'Why don't you go home, Lydia, and I'll call you later?'

She stubbed out the cigarette on the top of the car.

'Are you and Sara going to the other crime scenes?'

'We are,' Sara said as she joined us. 'But they've both been cleaned up.'

Lydia smiled at her. 'Lead the way, Detective Inspector Rose.'

She got into the car before I could protest, fiddling with the radio as I sat in the passenger side. Late night music drifted out of the speakers as she started the engine; the Cocteau Twins' ephemeral tones serenaded us as Lydia followed Sara out of the estate.

'Are you okay?' I said as we left the flashing blue lights behind.

'How did you get used to it, Frank?'

'Get used to what?'

'The death, misery and the suffering.'

I pressed my fingers into my legs. 'You never get used to it, Lydia. You bottle up the pain and store it somewhere it can do the least damage.'

She shook her head. 'That can't be good for you.'

I shrugged. 'It isn't, but it's better than confronting your emotions every time you encounter the horrors of human behaviour.'

Silence engulfed us as she kept up with Sara, driving away from Stanport and back towards Billsdale. My home-town separated the two coastal resorts, and as we passed it, I thought of my father in the hospital, wondering how long it would be before I was standing over his dead body.

'I didn't know what Uncle Tony was doing with the kids his thugs abducted in Whiteport.'

Tony Thompson, my former schoolmate – not that he was ever my mate – and Lydia's uncle: the drug baron of Whiteport and the surrounding area, who also got his goons to kidnap refugee children for bare-knuckle fights where several of them died.

'I never thought you did, Lydia. So don't worry about it.'

I watched her grip the steering wheel, so her fingers turned white.

'But I do, Frank. Every time I go to sleep, I see those kids' faces peering at me.' She looked at me as she drove. 'That's why I want to know how you deal with all the bad things you've seen.'

I had no answer to her beyond the one I'd already given, but I knew we'd need to have a longer conversation about it after tonight.

Once we visited two more places where people I'd never met were tortured and killed.

8 COUNTRY DEATH SONG

The second victim's house overlooked the sea in Billsdale. I stood outside as Sara spoke to Lydia, guessing the conversation was about me as I gazed at the waves lapping at the wall. The turbines were lit up in the water, blinking away like the Martian machines in *War of the Worlds*.

The wind blew fret and sand at me as I turned towards the house. The building was detached from the other houses on both sides, the gaps big enough to drive a car through. I scanned the area, searching for anything that might have caught the killers in action. There were internet cameras further down the seafront, and I hoped there would be some there, even though I knew the police would have covered that possibility. Sara must have read my mind.

'No CCTV, Frank, and none of the neighbours or anybody else saw or heard anything.'

I peered at the front of the property, seeing a nondescript building similar to others along the stretch. Looking directly over the beach and into the sea, its location would have added a considerable amount to its price. I wondered if its position as a "murder house" would increase or decrease its value.

'How long had the victim lived here?' I said.

'Harold Burke and his wife had a million-pound house in Whiteport until he retired a decade ago and moved here,' Sara said.

I tried to imagine what it would be like to have such wealth. I was raised on a council estate in a family that owned nothing; even the television was rented.

'He was a solicitor?'

She nodded. 'For forty years.'

'And the wife was away at a writing retreat with her friends when Burke was murdered?'

'She has a perfect alibi if you're thinking of her as a killer, Frank.'

'Aren't you considering her? With the murder of a husband or wife, the spouse is usually the number one suspect.'

Sara laughed as the chill of the night bit at my face.

'Apart from witnesses placing her twenty miles from the crime scene, Mrs Burke is seventy-five years old and is hardly the type to crucify somebody upside down.'

Lydia stepped between us, her purple suit dazzling my eyes in the encroaching gloom.

'She might have paid someone to kill her husband. I hear it happens all the time.'

Sara shook her head. 'Get your ears cleaned, Lydia. There's no connection between the three victims, including their families.'

I pulled my jacket closer to my chest. 'Let's have a look inside.'

Sara removed keys from her pocket, walked up the steps, and opened the front door. We followed her into a short corridor. I pointed at the keys, assuming they contained ones for the first victim's house.

'Did you know you'd be giving me a tour tonight before calling me?'

She shrugged. 'I told you, Frank; once we found your name in Cash's stomach, the Chief Constable was adamant I take you to the crime scenes to see if anything sparks your brain into motion.'

I peered at the photo frames on the walls. 'We better get started, then.'

Sara led us through the house, so I stared into a stranger's rooms and peered into what had been their life. There were no memories of Burke's time as a solicitor, only photos and mementoes of his time with his wife. Reading appeared to have been his favourite hobby, with most places stuffed with overflowing paperback and hardback bookshelves. In the living room was an extensive collection of local history books, going right back to Billsdale's origins as a fishing hamlet in the fourteenth century. I grabbed a hardback and flicked through it, staring at old black and white photographs of the pier and Victorian boats. Somebody, Burke probably, had scribbled notes on the pages, but it was impossible to decipher the scrawl.

I returned the book to the shelf. 'Was he a local historian, Sara?'

She had a copy of *Jude the Obscure* in her hand. 'I think he just enjoyed reading, going by what's here.'

Lydia laughed. 'You're right; I see dozens of Mills and Boon novels.'

I stared at the one she had in her hand, the cover showing a woman swooning in the arms of a shirtless, muscular man.

'Perhaps they're Mrs Burke's books.'

Lydia scowled at me. 'Don't be sexist, Frank. Men like romance as well.'

Sara laughed. 'Not the ones I've met.'

Lydia grinned at her. 'You just haven't met the right bloke, Sara.' She nodded at me. 'But there's still time.'

I ignored the jab and went upstairs. An eerie glow lit the rooms, electric rays spreading as petals upon the walls. The shadows danced through the bedrooms as I checked every nook and cranny, peering into each wardrobe and chest of drawers. Nothing jumped out at me; there were no signs calling out my name or indicating why somebody had murdered the owner in such a horrible way.

After spending fifteen minutes there, I returned to the others downstairs.

'This is pointless. There's nothing in this house that means anything to me.'

Sara looked downhearted. 'Are you sure?'

'I'm positive.' I moved to the door. 'How far away is the farm of the first victim?'

'It's twenty minutes' drive. Do you want to see where Burke was crucified before we leave?'

I didn't, but I said yes anyway.

She took us out of the living room and into the dining area. A large wooden table with four chairs stood in the middle, cupboards and shelves clinging to the walls. I searched for a space wide enough to nail a human body, but there wasn't one.

'Where was he killed?'

Sara pointed at the table. 'Whoever did it turned that upside down and nailed Burke to it.'

I moved closer to the table, examining it and seeing the holes where the nails had been punched into it. And the dried bloodstains around them.

'Eeww,' Lydia said. 'I wouldn't want to eat off that now. Does Burke's wife know?'

Sara nodded. 'I'm not sure she'll live here again. I wouldn't.'

I ran my fingers over the table, feeling the old wood bristle against my skin. It was thick, heavy, and likely a two-person job to turn it over and prop it against the wall. And then to get Burke upside down and nailed to it.

'What do you think, Frank?' Sara said.

'They must have covered his mouth to stop him from screaming.'

'And they knew his wife would be away,' Lydia said.

I thought of her with her friends when she heard about her husband's murder.

'How long did he take to die?'

'Between six to ten hours, according to the pathologist.'

'Was he tortured beforehand?'

'Yes,' Sara said. 'But there was no flogging. Instead, whoever did it used knives from the kitchen to remove Burke's skin.'

Lydia placed a hand on her cheek. 'All of it?'

Sara shook her head. 'No, only from his face and torso. Perhaps they didn't have time to do the rest.'

We stood there in silence, and I guessed they were trying to do the same as me, to erase that image from our minds but failing.

'I'll take you to the Baker farm,' Sara said.

We followed her out of the house. Drizzle drifted through the air as we reached Lydia's car.

'I wonder what Mrs Burke will do with all those books?' Lydia said as she started the engine. 'There must be thousands in there.'

I let her think about that as she drove away from the sea.

There was no apparent connection between Cash and Burke, and neither of them meant anything to me.

So why was my name inside Cash's stomach?

Perhaps the scene of the first victim might answer that.

Lydia followed Sara out of the town and onto a narrow road. As we entered the countryside, she drove past cottages and farmhouses. The woods were ahead as we passed a farmstead advertising fresh eggs for sale and another with a bed-and-breakfast notice outside. We left those behind and headed up a dirt track flanked on either side by large towering trees. I'd seen no sign leading to the Baker farm, so unless you knew it was there or got lost and stumbled upon it by accident, there would have been little chance of finding it without prior knowledge.

Which meant the killers knew where Baker had lived.

Killers. I kept thinking that and Sara had used the term, but was it possible one person could have committed those three murders? Could a single individual have positioned the victims upside down to nail their hands and feet to the wall? Or, in Burke's case, to that table? I suppose it was conceivable if they were strong enough, but it seemed unlikely. Yet it couldn't be ruled out. I'd seen former colleagues in the Met dismiss possible suspects because they didn't fit their preconceived idea of who the killer was to know it was a dangerous path to take.

We rounded a bend and pulled up outside a small farmhouse. As I got out of the car, I couldn't see any other buildings and wondered if it was a working farm or somewhere Baker had gone to enjoy his retirement.

All three victims were retired – did that mean anything?

Moreover, why was I even thinking like that? I wasn't a copper or investigator anymore, only doing this as a favour for Sara. And she'd been forced to get me there because of her Chief Constable.

She opened the front door and took us inside, straight into a homely-looking living room of oversized sofas, rugs, a rocking chair and a large open fireplace. It would have been nice to see it lit since it was as cold there as it had been outside.

'Robert Baker moved here thirty years ago after leaving the NHS. It was a working farm then, mainly dairy products and supplying fresh meat to local businesses, but he had people working on it.

I glanced around the room, my guts grumbling and imagining a bacon sandwich in my hand.

'Did he have any family?'

'His wife died twelve years ago. Their daughter moved away just after to continue her studies.'

I listened to her while staring at the large space on the far wall, seeing the marks and stains.

I pointed at it. 'Is that where they crucified him?'

Sara nodded. 'Same as the other two, though, according to the pathologist, Baker wasn't tortured.'

My legs ached, so I sat on the closest sofa, peering at the wall and picturing Baker pinned upside down as the blood seeped out of him, and he slowly ran out of breath.

'Crucifixion is an unusual method of murder,' I said. 'Even more so when it's done with the victim upside down, so there has to be a meaning there.' I looked at Sara as she scrutinised me. 'Have you discovered anything about that?'

She took a single seat opposite me. 'I've done my research, Frank if that's what you meant.'

Lydia spoke as she glanced through Baker's record collection. 'It's a religious thing, isn't it?'

'I'll tell you what I found online,' Sara said. 'The Cross

of Saint Peter or Petrine Cross is an inverted Latin cross, traditionally used as a Christian symbol but also as an anti-Christian symbol in recent times. In Christianity, it's associated with the martyrdom of Peter the Apostle. The symbol originates from the Catholic tradition that when sentenced to death, Peter requested his cross be upside down, as he felt unworthy of being crucified in the same manner as Jesus.'

Something sharp stabbed at my chest. 'Do you believe these murders are religiously motivated, Sara?'

'I'm unsure about the motive, but it's hard to argue against the method having a religious connection. It's the first thing the Chief Constable said to me after Baker's body was discovered in this room.'

I glanced over her shoulder at that space on the wall.

'Is the Chief Constable a religious man?'

She smiled at me. 'There's a Bible on his desk and another in the glove compartment of his car.'

'God's cop then?'

'I guess you could say that.'

I assumed there were several things she couldn't tell me about this investigation. Still, my curiosity forced me to ask her about something that was bothering me.

'One murder at Stanport and two at Billsdale, but you're stationed at Whiteport. So, why you, Sara?'

'It's simple; the Chief Constable knows of my friendship with you.'

'Yet you only found my name with the third victim. Haven't you been on this investigation from the start?'

'I have. Frank, it's no big conspiracy, so don't get any daft ideas. In the last decade, cut-backs have led to the local closure of a dozen police stations and losing more than a thousand experienced officers.'

'Didn't the government promise to increase police

numbers?'

She laughed at me. 'I realise you retired from the force last year, Frank, but you can't have forgotten how the world works. Politicians guarantee the earth to get your vote, but you don't matter once they have it. There'll be no new hospitals, schools or coppers around here until it becomes a political necessity. In this case, that's what I am, a necessity, nothing more or less. If we'd had more staff, I wouldn't be with you now, but for better or worse, I'm the most experienced detective we have.

'And you've kept these murders from the media?'

'Not the deaths, no. They were reported, but we didn't release any gory details. The Chief Constable doesn't like the idea of the media running stories with headlines that scream Crucifix Killer on the Loose.'

'The Upside Down Crucifix Killer,' Lydia said.

Sara rubbed at her head. 'Christ, that's all we need.' She laughed as she realised what she'd said. 'No pun intended.' Then she looked straight at me. 'You got nothing from here.'

I watched Lydia picking out record sleeves as I answered. 'No. This place, and Baker, is as much a mystery to me as the others.'

'Perhaps the Crucifix Killer is a collector,' Lydia said.

Sara grimaced at the use of that name. 'What do you mean?'

Lydia held a John Coltrane album in front of her. 'Well, aren't all serial killers collectors of some sort? Don't they take trophies to remind them of their victims?'

'A lot do,' I said as I turned to Sara. 'Have you noticed anything missing from the crime scenes?'

She shook her head. 'We haven't, but that doesn't mean to say Lydia isn't right.'

'What's in his record collection, Lydia?' I said.

She replaced the Coltrane album and flicked through the others.

'Miles Davis, Charlie Parker, Duke Ellington, Dizzy Gillespie; that kind of stuff.'

I pulled a face at her.

'Something wrong, Frank?' Sara said.

I laughed. 'I'm allergic to jazz.'

Lydia scowled at me. 'You're a philistine, Walker.'

'That's untrue, my friend. I just focus on the music I grew up with.'

Lydia moved from the records and nearer to me. 'Which is what?'

I reached into my brain for the tunes of my youth. 'The Happy Mondays; 808 State; Orbital; Primal Scream.'

'Never heard of them,' Lydia said, though I assumed she was joking. 'I thought all coppers loved jazz? Every time I read crime fiction, the detective is always a jazz-loving alkie with a terrible history with women.'

I shrugged. 'One out of three isn't bad. Still, most of my colleagues in the Met were jazz aficionados, just like some were misogynists, racists and homophobes. And things didn't get better when the government put a woman in charge.'

They stared at me, probably expecting a rant, but I was too tired for that. We'd visited three crime scenes and found nothing to connect me to the victims. I didn't know if that was a good thing, but Sara was obviously disappointed.

'You don't see any connection between Baker and you?'

'I'm afraid not.'

I wasn't afraid at all. Far from it, I was glad. We left the farmhouse, and I pushed all thoughts of crucifix killings out of my mind.

Now I had to focus on what to do with my father.

9 THIS CHARMING MAN

I spent a sleepless night once Lydia dropped me off. I should have been used to being on my own, but it felt strange in the family home while the old man was in the hospital, unsure if he'd ever come back.

After showering the next morning, I headed into the kitchen for breakfast, my stomach rumbling louder than a volcano about to explode. As I opened the fridge, I remembered I hadn't been shopping for two days, finding cheese that shouldn't have been blue and some unknown meat that wouldn't have passed any food safety standards.

I filled the kettle: a mug of tea would have to do until I went into town and found somewhere to eat. I couldn't turn up at the hospital on an empty stomach. While waiting for the water to boil, I sat at the table and checked my phone for messages, happy to find there weren't any. Then I opened the internet, browsing for any mention of the Crucifix Killer. There was nothing apart from two lines on a local website reporting on the discovery of David Cash's body, but with none of the gory details. I flicked through it, but knew it wouldn't be long before the media got hold of the story and splashed it all over the news. It surprised me they hadn't already, wondering if the God-fearing Chief Constable had had anything to do with that.

As the water boiled, I glanced at the national headlines online, pausing as the steam erupted into the room to see it was the same headline on every major site: a serving officer in the Metropolitan Police had been caught exposing himself in a London park.

I let the kettle boil and read the details, remembering my last week as a Met officer: the teenager who'd died on a park bench from respiratory failure; the female pensioner whose partially decomposed body a neighbour found in her bedroom; the alcoholic who choked on his own vomit; the fourteen-year-old girl discovered strangled in a dumpster; and the middle-aged man who'd jumped from the tenth floor of a block of high-rise flats, leaving behind a wife and two young children. Not all of them were my investigations, but I knew all the officers involved.

Was I thinking of them as an excuse for the copper found wanking in a London park? No, of course not. They sprang back into my mind because I expected to go to the hospital and learn my father didn't have long to live. So I was preparing myself for the inevitable by getting acquainted with death again.

I made the tea and filled the mug with sugar at that table I'd sat at forty years before. The kitchen had hardly changed since then, apart from the new electrical goods I'd bought a few weeks after returning home. I pictured the out-of-date cheese in the fridge as I took my drink upstairs, using the time to change the sheets on the old man's bed. I consumed enough sugar to destroy my teeth in one go as I tried not to think that he might never return.

I placed the mug on the window ledge as I stripped the

bedsheets. As I did, I noticed the photo albums under the bed and bent down to remove them. The bed creaked as I sat on it, opening an album and staring at the first picture. It was one I'd seen many times before, but it still affected me every time I saw it: my parents' black and white wedding photo. He wore an enormous smile, but my mother's was hardly present, just a slight upturn of her top lip. I'd always assumed that was because she was three months pregnant with my eldest sister, but perhaps it was the realisation of what the future held for her.

My back ached as I pushed it into the frame of the bed, flicking through those photos I'd seen many times before: the older sisters I had little memory of; my brother before I was born, dressed like a cowboy and pointing a gun at the camera, a prescient image of what waited for him when he got older. There were a few pictures of me, all as a baby or when I was primary school age. I wasn't smiling in any of them and didn't remember when they were taken.

I closed the album and replaced all of them under the bed. I'd never been one for nostalgia or reminiscing, and this wasn't the time to start. I finished the tea and put the new covers and sheets on. At least it would be presentable when the old man returned.

If he returned.

When I got downstairs, the phone rang, my mobile vibrating on the kitchen table. I left it there, twisting and turning as if an angry demon possessed it. I gazed at the table, picturing the one on which they had crucified Harold Burke. Against my better judgement, I'd been thinking about the case and who would commit such crimes.

I grabbed the phone to see it was Lydia calling. She didn't seem happy when I answered.

'You took your time, Walker.'

'Is it an emergency?'

'No, but you know how impatient I get.'

Did I know that? Even with the age difference, we'd become good friends since she'd returned from abroad, but considering I'd convinced her to help put her Uncle Tony behind bars, there were still plenty of things I didn't know about her. And that was how it should have been, apart from the fact that last night I'd discovered she liked jazz.

'Don't tell me you've bought tickets for us to see Ed Sheeran in concert?'

She snorted down the phone. 'What? God, no. I'd rather be crucified upside down than put up with that.'

'Well, being a jazz fan, I wasn't sure what you're capable of.'

'You're lucky I'm not there with you, Frank, or I'd strangle you with my bare hands.'

'Okay, enough with the death threats. Why are you calling?'

'I guess you got out of the wrong side of the bed this morning.'

She was correct; I had snapped at her. 'Sorry, Lydia. I didn't get a lot of sleep last night.'

'Did visiting those murder scenes affect you, Frank?'

Had they? I hoped it was they and not me worrying about the old man.

'No, it wasn't that. They're nothing to do with me. Sara can handle them.'

'You're not curious about your name being on a piece of paper inside the guts of the last victim?'

Of course I was, but I wouldn't admit it to her.

'It doesn't mean anything, Lydia. I'm guessing the killers did it just to wind up the police. It could have been anybody's name on that paper.'

She laughed before she spoke. 'Surely you don't believe that, Frank?'

'I've got other things to worry about.'

She didn't reply for twenty seconds. 'Yeah, I know. That's why I'm ringing. Do you need a lift to the hospital?'

I glanced at the clock on the wall. Visiting time was an hour away, but I didn't want to monopolise Lydia's time again. And maybe I just wanted to be on my own with my thoughts today.

'No, that's okay, thanks. I'll get a taxi there. I might go for a walk in the park nearby after seeing the old man.'

'Is that the one where you got stuck up the tree as a kid and your mother had to call the fire brigade to get you down?'

I felt the heat rise over my neck. 'How do you know about that?'

She laughed again. 'Your dad told me a few weeks ago. I know all your childhood secrets, Walker, so you better be nice to me in the future.'

'I'm always nice to you, Thompson. Even when you don't deserve it.'

Lydia continued laughing before ending the call. I laughed as well as I phoned for a taxi to take me to the hospital.

THIRTY MINUTES LATER, I was sitting outside his room, waiting to speak to Dr Kitty Carlisle. The ward sister who'd met me at the desk had said the old man was doing okay, but I hadn't seen him yet.

'You look terrible, Frank.'

I looked up to see Kitty striding towards me.

'You certainly know how to cheer a guy up.'

She smiled as she sat next to me. 'I'm worried about you. We don't want you getting ill when your father is getting better.'

I felt my heart lift inside my chest. 'He's improving?'

'He is, little by little, but we must have a serious discussion about his future.'

Then my heart sank again. 'His future?'

'We've spoken about this before, Frank. Your father might live for ten years or more, but he will need professional care sooner than later. What happened yesterday was only a reminder of that.'

I resisted the urge to take her hand, though some human contact wouldn't have gone amiss right then.

'Can I see him now?'

She got up. 'Of course. He's awake, but I'd like to keep him in for at least one more night if that's okay with you?'

I agreed and followed her into his room.

He didn't talk much, but I sat with him for an hour. There was no mention of what happened to him, but he was interested in what had ensued at the community centre party.

His false teeth rattled in his mouth as he grinned at me. 'I think that woman fancied you, Frank.'

'Eva Cross?'

'That's the one. She's probably desperate to get back here from Australia. It's full of convicts, you know.'

He laid there, chuntering as I thought of Eva. And of Kitty Carlisle, nearby. Wasn't my life complicated enough without starting a relationship?

Then I pictured my name on that paper inside David Cash's guts.

He wouldn't be the first person who couldn't stomach me.

I laughed at my poor attempt at humour as the old man dozed off. I left him sleeping and looked for Kitty outside, but a nurse told me she'd been called away to see another patient. It was probably a good thing, as I'd likely have made a fool of myself by asking her out.

I exited the hospital, turning up the road, heading towards the park where I'd spent much of my youth. It was brimming with fresh flowers when I arrived, the smell of rosewood and lavender filling the air. A large lake was in the middle, with families and young kids surrounding it. Several dogs yapped at each other as I strode to the benches outside the café at the top.

My legs throbbed as I wondered when I'd got so unfit. I'd thought about joining Lydia on her early morning runs along the beach, but her place was ten miles from where I lived, so it would mean getting up earlier than I would have liked. Still, it would be nice to have an exercise routine to get me into shape. And I was sure she wouldn't laugh at me too much.

I considered that as I peered across the park, searching out the tree I'd climbed all those years ago. It was still there, staring back at me, mocking me with its withered branches as I imagined its voice in my head.

You were fourteen, and I'm not even that tall – so how did you get stuck?

I'd panicked, that's why. Once I got up there, I lost my nerve when I saw the ground below me.

And ever since then, I'd tried not to do the same.

Because once you lose your nerve, there's no going back.

I was still staring into the trees when my phone rang.

'Are you calling to give me bad news, Sara?'

'Possibly. How's your dad, Frank?'

I pictured myself jumping out of that tree thirty years ago, something that only happened in my mind then and now.

'He should come home soon.' I don't know why I told her that. 'Then things will be back to normal.' I wasn't sure if I even knew what normal was anymore. 'Has there been a development in the case?'

I heard her take a deep breath. 'Have you seen the news?'

'Only briefly this morning. Your team is doing a good job of keeping the gruesome details from the media.'

'That's all about to disappear, Frank. The SIO, Detective Chief Inspector Coe, is about to give a media conference.'

'DCI Coe is the Senior Investigating Officer? Is he or she a long-distance runner?'

'No, but I think he's lining you up for the high jump.'

It was my turn to take a deep breath. 'He thinks I'm involved in these murders?'

'You are involved. Or have you forgotten we found the words Frank Walker inside the stomach of the last victim?'

'How could I, Sara? I can still picture his house from yesterday.' I pushed the images into the shadows where I'd stored the memories of every crime scene I'd seen over the years. 'Will Coe mention my name at this news conference?'

'I asked him not to, but I'm not sure how much he listens to me.'

'You don't get along with him?'

'How many of your senior officers did you get along with at the Met, Frank?'

I thought of my former colleagues, considering how few I was still in touch with after returning north.

'Is that why you've called, Sara, to warn me I might be all over the news this afternoon?'

There was the sound of somebody speaking to her in the background. Then she swore at them.

'Sorry, Frank; that wasn't for you.'

I laughed as kids kicked a ball around in the park. 'No problem. I assume it's tense over there.'

'Just a bit. That's why I need you to come to the station.'

A young lad threw the football, hitting his mate square in the face. The teenager dropped to the ground while the rest of them burst out laughing.

'Why, Sara?'

'Coe wants you to give a statement about what you know of the three victims, especially the last one, David Cash.'

'Didn't you tell him I've never met or heard of them?'

'He needs to hear it from you face to face, Frank.' Her

pause told me there was bad news on the way. 'He's spoken to several of your former Met colleagues.'

I watched as the lad got up from the ground, wiping at the blood streaming from his nose.

'These would be the same people you spoke to, Sara, not long before we first met?'

'Probably some of them.'

'The ones who gave you nothing but ringing endorsements about me?'

'All of them said what a good copper you were, Frank. I'm sure they'll have told DCI Coe the same.' The lads had stopped playing football and were arguing with each other, their voices reaching me. 'Are you in a pub?'

'If only. When does he want me at the station?'

'As soon as possible. The media announcement will be over by the time you arrive.'

'And that will have put him in such a good mood.'

'It's only a formality, Frank. Get it over and done with, and that will be that.'

'Sure, Sara. I'll see you soon.'

I ended the call and went onto the internet to find a live broadcast of Coe's news conference. Seeing him in action might prepare me better for the grilling I'd likely receive. It didn't take long for the links to pop up on several social media sites, and I clicked on the one for the local newspaper. I'd missed the start, observing DCI Coe in his uniform, standing in front of a table and reading from a prepared statement. Even watching through a tiny mobile phone with the camera only focused on him, I could sense the air being sucked out of the room as he listed the barest details regarding the murders. He seemed younger than me, perhaps in his late thirties, with no emotion on his face as he described how the men died.

'Crucified upside down.'

They were the three words I assumed would reverberate around the country in seconds. He continued speaking to his audience, not yet taking questions from the unseen journalists. I speculated if any of them knew the third victim, the former journalist, David Cash.

Then I wondered if he'd mention my name.

If this case had happened under the Met's supervision when I was there, we wouldn't have mentioned that type of detail at this stage when informing the public. It was something, for now, that only needed to be known by those who'd committed the crimes and those trying to solve them.

I waited as Coe finished, happy that my name never came up as the DCI took questions from the audience. The first one didn't surprise me.

'Do you have any leads on the Crucifix Killer?'

The media had already decided the perpetrator was a single individual. I listened to Coe answer the question by not answering it, imagining Lydia shouting at her TV screen that it was the Upside Down Crucifix Killer.

I'd seen and heard enough, closing the internet and putting the phone in my pocket. As I left the park, the teenagers were playing football again, and I glanced one last time to that tree that had contained me so many years ago. I walked to the police station, past the hospital and through places I'd frequented when I was a teenager. There were modern houses and new shops, but I saw the same types of residents I remembered from my youth: kids with nowhere to go and nothing to do, suddenly realising there was no future for them beyond existing at the lowest end of society. That's if society was a concept they understood or recognised. Then there were the adults, not much better off than the children, just further along on the journey to oblivion.

On the surface, the estates lacked only investment and encouragement, but I could sense the flow of alcohol, drugs and crime lingering nearby.

Once out of the area, I was into Whiteport town centre. It was a lengthy main road to the shopping centre, a building built in the early 1970s that looked the same as when I was a troublesome teenager shoplifting from its stores. I didn't go inside, but the memories were still there, unlike most of the shops that had long since gone the way of the dinosaurs: Rumbelows; Tandy; Dixons; and Woolworths. I'd stolen from all of their shelves and had lasted into the twenty-first century longer than they had.

I didn't seep into nostalgia at their loss, but I missed those places whose products had helped me grow into adulthood: the record shops where I bought my first albums and singles; and the bookshops that had extended my knowledge of fantastic fiction.

After that, it wasn't long before I reached the police station, just beyond the town's railway station. It had been built long after I'd left for London, so it wasn't the place where plainclothes officers had tried to intimidate me when I was caught shoplifting as a teenager. Their threats of terrible things happening if I continued my criminal ways never bothered me. I didn't have to worry about what would be said at home because my parents weren't interested in anything their children did, even when it was lawbreaking.

Those memories lingered inside my head as I approached the station, unsurprised to see several media vehicles and groups of journalists outside the front. They ignored me as I walked into the building, stopping at reception to ask for DI Rose. As I waited, I peered out the window, seeing more cars and vans adorned with the symbols of the biggest news channels joining the others.

'We've gone global, Frank.' There was no joy in Sara's voice or her face. 'But at least the media don't know who you are.'

And how long would it stay like that?

'Where's Coe?' I said.

'Follow me,' Sara said.

She led me through the central area, beyond the officers and civilian staff doing their jobs, and into a windowless room at the back. The man I'd seen on the internet giving the news conference was sitting at a table waiting for us.

He was waiting for me.

Coe didn't get up. 'DI Rose has told me so much about you, Mr Walker. I'm Detective Chief Inspector Simon Coe.'

He didn't offer me his hand, and I didn't move from the doorway.

'Call me Frank.'

Sara pulled a chair for me to sit on, so I did. Coe smiled at me.

'DI Rose recorded her conversations with you last night, Frank, so we have a record of your claim not to know David Cash, Harold Burke, and Robert Baker, the three victims of a killer, or killers, in this county during the last two weeks.'

I glanced from her to him. 'If that's so, why am I here now?'

'I've spoken to several of your former colleagues in the Metropolitan Police, Frank, and studied the case that led to your resignation from the Met.' His smile disappeared. 'And some things I've heard are concerning, considering your link to the latest victim, David Cash.'

'Concerning how?' I said.

'The people who know you the best,' he said. 'Those who worked closely with you for several years told me you always liked to put yourself at the centre of every investigation.' He stared straight at me, his eyes unmoving. 'It was as if you needed to be the focus of attention. Isn't that why you were forced out of the Met?'

I looked at Sara, but she glanced away. Had she known Coe would take this line with me?

'What's this got to do with the Crucifix Killer?' I said.

His expression finally changed. 'Please don't use that term. It's a media construction we aren't comfortable with.'

'I apologise for making you uncomfortable, Coe.'

He placed one hand on the table, and I noticed his perfectly manicured nails.

'Your name was discovered on a piece of paper in the stomach of the latest victim. Don't you think that's strange?'

I shrugged. 'Sure, but no stranger than the popularity of Jimmy Carr or the Conservative Party. There's no accounting for some things in this world.'

'So you have no suggestions for why your name was inside David Cash's guts?'

I shook my head. 'Do I need a lawyer?'

'No, Frank,' Sara said. 'We just need a formal record of your statement stating you've never met the three victims.'

I stood, quelling the annoyance rising in me. 'Well, you've got it now.'

Coe flashed me a smile reminiscent of a shark about to devour an unsuspecting swimmer.

'The public thinks you're a hero, Walker because you sacrificed your career to find where a serial killer buried the bodies of his victims, but that's not the case, is it?'

That serial killer was Christopher Matthews, and it seemed as if I'd never be able to put his crimes behind me.

'I'm sure you'll enlighten me.'

DCI Coe moved in for the kill. 'I have it on good

authority from your former colleagues that you were having a nervous breakdown at the time because your wife had left you. So when you spoke to Matthews at the river, you were already losing the plot. It wasn't about getting justice for the victims and their families, but a way for you to feel relevant again. Isn't that true?'

'True? Lies sound like facts to those conditioned to mis-recognise the truth.'

'You didn't expect them to accept your resignation, Walker. You thought that stellar reputation you carry around inside your head would have had the Met begging you to stay with them.' He grinned at me. 'But it never worked out like that.'

'You want to know why I left the Met? It's a bunch of donkeys led by nematodes. And not very bright ones at that.'

He narrowed his eyes at me, and I assumed it was because he didn't know what a nematode was.

'Some of my colleagues think if your ego was that fragile then, what must it be like now?' He glanced at Sara, who'd avoided my gaze the whole time. 'Perhaps you're so desperate for more recognition you need to be involved in a case involving another serial killer, especially one as extreme as this crucifix murderer.'

I laughed at him. 'You seriously can't be this deranged, Coe, to think I'm looking for public recognition by involving myself with a serial killer?'

He shrugged. 'Why not? You did it with Christopher Matthews, and when you returned to your home town, you made friends with a local gangster.'

'Tony Thompson? If you've forgotten, I helped put him behind bars and ended his criminal organisation. You can thank me for that any time you want.'

'You're still friendly with his niece. Isn't that true?'

'Lydia? I looked after her cat while she was away. That's it.'

'Are you sure? My information is that she accompanied you to all three murder scenes. And on your insistence.'

'Sara knows the reason for that,' I said. Finally, I'd had enough, turning to leave.

'We'll be monitoring you, Walker,' Coe said.

I left the office with DI Rose following me.

'I'm sorry about that, Frank.'

'Did you know what he'd say to me, Sara?'

She shook her head. 'No. He's under a lot of pressure about this. Of course, we all are, but I don't know why he thinks you're involved.'

'Apart from my name being on a piece of paper inside the last victim's stomach?'

'Well, yeah, apart from that.'

We stared at each other for thirty seconds before Coe shouted for Sara. I left without a goodbye, walking through the station with every eye on me. How many thought I was connected to the murders? Or that I was the killer? Most of them, probably. So many idiots join the police, and a few even climb the ranks to be chief constables.

I walked home, forgetting about crucified victims and dopey coppers, and focused on what I'd do about my father, wondering what he'd be like when he got out of the hospital.

If he got out of the hospital.

11   FOOD FOR THOUGHT

The following day the rain did its best to batter me into submission. I'd left the old man's umbrella at home because there'd been nothing but sunshine as far as the eye could see when I'd stepped out of the front door. Then, as I crossed the bridge over the train line, the heavens sprang a leak. Only it turned into more, an apocalyptic shower that might have been heralding God's disappointment in me and the three murders DCI Coe seemed convinced I knew something about.

Not that I believed in God or an afterlife. My parents were never religious until later in life, especially my mother, so maybe that crutch would come to me when I approached my own mortality, but I had no use for it now. Having an umbrella or even a hooded top would have been more helpful.

I could have turned back and went home, but Lydia had driven to Whiteport so I could take her for lunch. And I owed her for having put her through the nightmare of visiting the murder scenes. I also assumed she wanted an update on my visit to the police station.

So I trudged through the rain with Jim Morrison's voice in my head and images of my name on a bloodied piece of paper sticking to the back of my eyes. I hadn't checked the internet, so I didn't know how the media was dealing with the news Coe had sprung upon them yesterday. And I wondered how long it would be before somebody leaked the details of my connection to the latest victim.

Connection. No, there wasn't one between Cash and me or the others, no matter how hard I looked. I'd trawled the internet all night, searching for information on the victims, repeating, I guessed, what the police and journalists had already done, finding no link between Burke, Baker and Cash. And not a single connection with me. It was only when I woke at five in the morning that I wondered if the link was with my family?

I thought about visiting my father in the hospital and asking him if he knew any of the victims. However, I quickly dismissed the idea. I didn't want to disturb him while he was recovering. And because it sounded ludicrous. Once he'd been demobbed after the war, he spent all his working life driving trucks delivering oil and gas while living on a council estate. The chance of him meeting a journalist, solicitor, or farmer seemed remote to me. He probably delivered to farms, but would Baker's have been one of them? And Sara had said that Baker bought his farm thirty years ago, and I was sure the old man had retired by then. Even if he wasn't, would he remember anything from that time?

These thoughts pinged around inside my brain as the rain bounced off my head. I crossed the train line, staring at the point where the police had caught me and other kids throwing stones at a train decades ago. I was seven years old and couldn't say then or now why I did it. Perhaps it was just to go along with the others, but I'd never seen myself as somebody who bowed down to peer pressure or for being part of a crowd.

I left that behind and came off the bridge, stepping into a row of shops and heading for the café at the end. We could have met anywhere, but Lydia chose it, and I didn't argue. Her car was outside, parked somewhere it shouldn't have been. She was sitting near the window when I went inside, dropping several sugar cubes into a large mug of tea.

'Your full English breakfast is on its way, Frank.'

I sat opposite her. 'I hope you told them fried tomatoes, not tinned stuff.' My jaw ached as I grimaced. 'I've got childhood nightmares from having to eat that muck. Tinned vegetables and tinned fruit are alien concepts to me.'

'Well, Mr Walker, not everyone has your delicate tastes.' She pushed a bottle of brown sauce towards me. 'And for those living on the breadline, tinned food is much more practical and cheaper than buying fresh mangoes and courgettes daily.'

'Mango and courgette sound like the worst pizza toppings ever.'

Lydia shook her head. 'No, that would be anchovies.'

I noticed the newspaper in front of her. 'Speaking of things to make you sick, why are you reading *The Daily Fail*?'

She shrugged. 'It was here when I arrived, and I wanted to see what they were reporting about the crucifix murders. Don't worry, I'll take a hot bath and fumigate my clothes when I get home.'

A woman brought me a mug of steaming tea, and I used it to push the paper from me.

'So, what is the nation's poor excuse for journalists

saying about our local serial killers? Are they blaming immigrants?'

Lydia warmed her fingers on her mug. 'There's no mention of killers, only the Crucifix Killer.'

I nodded. 'We always knew that would be the name they'd use, whether it's accurate or not.'

'I guess that Upside Down Crucifix Killer wouldn't fit as a headline without making the text too small to read.'

I pointed at the paper. 'Did they enlighten the public on the grisly details of the crimes?'

The woman returned to the table, bringing large plates of sweet-smelling fried goodness. I covered mine with brown sauce as Lydia spoke.

'Whoever wrote the article must have delved between the lines of the police statement and extrapolated their own strange theories regarding the murders, ranging from roaming killer Satanists to loony left-wingers striking out against the bedrocks of conservatism.'

I crunched on a slice of delicious bacon. 'The bedrocks of conservatism?'

She grinned at me. 'A farmer, a solicitor, and a journalist.'

'Did Cash write for a right-wing newspaper?'

'Don't they all?' She didn't wait for an answer. 'Do you know what else I read in that excuse for a paper?'

'Nothing good.'

'You got that right, Frank. There's a rumour that the next James Bond might be black or, heavens above, gay.'

I let the tea wash the eggs down my throat. 'I'm not that up-to-date on popular culture, Lydia.' However, I could guess how such a thing would go down with some sections of the population.

She shook her head. 'Imagine getting that upset over fictional characters.'

'How upset?'

'The general tone was how much deeper must our innocent childhood companions be dragged into the cesspool of immorality by depraved liberal writers before the stains just won't wash out.' She laughed loud enough to scare the old couple sitting behind us. 'James Bond as an innocent childhood companion, really?'

I relaxed into the chair, happy not to think about my father's health or my name force-fed to a murder victim: an upside-down crucified victim.

'I don't mind some Bond movies, but I couldn't get away with the novels, finding them quite dated.'

'A gay James Bond gets my vote. Half of my male friends would audition for it.' She winked at me. 'Where will it all end, Frank? Cats marrying chickens? Spider and fly orgies? Children raised by robots?'

She raised her voice as she spoke, and I was sure it was to worry the old folks behind her.

'It's the end of the world as we know it, Lydia.' I stuck my fork into a sausage and then bit it in half. 'So we might as well enjoy it while we can.'

She narrowed her eyes. 'Tell me what happened at the cop shop.'

I finished my tea and relayed my time with Detective Chief Inspector Coe to her, including his ludicrous claims.

'I don't think DCI Coe is too enamoured with me.'

'And Sara just sat there saying nothing?'

'Not until I left, and she apologised for his stupidity.'

Lydia wiped beans from the plate with a slice of toast before dumping them into her mouth. She munched on her food as she spoke.

'Maybe he wasn't being stupid?'

'What?' I said. 'You believe I'm involved in the murders because I want to return to the limelight?'

'No, of course not. But perhaps there is a connection to you because of something in your past.'

'To do with my family?'

'Could be, but I was thinking more about you having childhood enemies who are now getting back at you in their own warped way.'

'This is more than warped, Lydia. What could I have done to anyone decades ago that would get them to crucify three men?'

'My uncle said you upset many people when you were a teenager, Frank. Might these murders have anything to do with that?'

I laughed at her. 'You think something I did as a kid has led to these crimes?'

She shrugged. 'I'm just throwing out theories until we have a better idea of what's happening.'

A glass of water was on the table, and I drank from it.

'If somebody is holding a grudge against me for thirty years and thinks it's worth killing for, I don't know what I did to wound someone that bad.'

She peered at me. 'Are you sure?'

I wasn't, but I didn't have the mental strength to trawl through my memories for any imagined slights.

'I can't remember much of my teenage years, Lydia. Most of it was unremarkable.'

'Who were your friends and your enemies? What about girlfriends? Did you get into any fights? Was there any trouble at school? I know you had a problem with your older brother, but what about your sisters and parents?'

The water hadn't erased the dryness in my mouth.

'It sounds like you've thought a lot about this, about my past.'

'I have an analytical mind, Frank. It's one reason Uncle Tony got me so involved in his business.'

'That might be true, Lydia, and this isn't a criticism, but he still kept secrets from you.'

'You mean the drug dealing, child abduction, and forcing teenagers into death fights? You're right, but perhaps I was too close to him to see what was happening under my nose, and I couldn't turn to the authorities. Like most people where I grew up, I deeply distrust the police. They've dragged me away from protests and demonstrations and intimidated my friends and me because of how we dressed or what we believed in. They threw my best friend in jail because she was ill. They harassed anybody who didn't stick to the status quo or who'd dared to come to this country from somewhere else. I was raised with a working-class suspicion of authority that is generations thick. So even when I saw Uncle Tony and his cronies breaking the law, I could tell myself it was better than trusting the coppers.'

She stopped talking as a couple entered the café.

I considered her words, not focusing on her upbringing – we might need to revisit that later – but more on what she'd said about me. Was it possible the crucifix murders had a connection to my past, linked to something I'd done years ago?

That idea possessed my mind as my phone rang. I looked at the screen as Lydia gazed at the dessert menu. Sara's name flickered on the mobile as I wondered whether to answer after what had happened with DCI Coe.

'Lemon meringue or sticky toffee pudding?' Lydia said.

I licked at my sweet tooth as I answered the call.

'Are you calling to apologise again, Sara?'

She wasn't.

'There's been another crucifix murder, Frank.'

12 PSYCHO KILLER

The village of Upper Slope was a twenty-minute drive away. It was only small, with a dozen houses, a dilapidated church, and a monument to the fallen of two world wars. When we arrived, everywhere was full of police cars, flickering red and blue lights turning the countryside into a daytime disco.

'This is the first time I've been here,' Lydia said as she parked at the end of the road.

'I used to cycle through here as a kid,' I said as I got out of the car. She scrutinised me. 'As did hundreds of others.'

We walked towards the flashing illuminations.

'Did you ever go into this house?'

I shook my head. 'No. This area was far too posh for me.' I glanced at the other houses. 'And it still is – these must be all million-pound properties.'

DI Rose was waiting for us in the street. 'You'll have to stay here, Lydia.'

She didn't argue. 'That's fine with me. Text me when you leave, Frank.'

'Where are you going?' I said.

She nodded towards the war memorial. 'I'm off to pay my respects.'

Sara handed me protection for my hands and feet.

'Have you been here before, Frank?'

'I told Lydia I cycled through here thirty years ago, but I haven't been back before now.'

Sara stared at me, and I wondered if something in that house was connected to me.

'I hope you've got a strong stomach.'

She led me past uniformed coppers and forensic specialists. The gaps to the neighbouring houses were wide enough so the people inside couldn't look out of the windows at what was happening.

I stepped into the house, and that familiar smell hit me like someone had set fire to a pile of copper. Officers glanced at me and then away as DI Rose led me into a large living room.

'Is this the same as the others, Sara?'

She nodded. 'But with one major difference: we have a witness.'

I stared at her in expectation. 'A relative of the victim?'

'The wife. The medics are with her upstairs. Somebody drugged her with ketamine, then blindfolded and bound her. She's in her seventies and frail, so they're about to take her to the hospital.'

'Has she said anything?'

'Not yet. It will probably have to wait until tomorrow.'

As I looked around the room, DCI Simon Coe approached.

'If it were up to me, you wouldn't be here, Walker.' The glint in his eyes from yesterday was long gone. 'But the Chief Constable thinks you're our only lead, so I'll put up with you for now.'

I ignored him, moving towards the body pinned to the wall. No, not pinned – crucified. The victim was upside down and nailed to the surface, but there was a significant difference to what Sara had told me about the first three victims — they'd sliced him open from the throat to the groin. His internal organs were hanging out of him like freshly made spaghetti. I put a hand to my nose to block the stink, but it didn't work.

Sara whispered to me. 'Don't throw up.'

'Did you find anything inside him?'

'Like your name?' Coe said.

I nodded. 'Or anything else unusual?'

'Not yet,' Sara said. 'We'll have to wait on the post-mortem.'

Against my better judgement and sense of smell, I moved closer to the body.

'Was he drugged?'

'We think so. We need to get the toxicology report, but I'd guess it was ketamine.'

I didn't ask if the police would check on ketamine dealers since anybody could get it over the internet through the dark web, where it would be impossible to trace. Instead, I inched nearer, peering at the man nailed upside down to the wall.

'It can't be easy getting the victims into this position.'

Sara moved next to me. 'You still think it might be more than one killer?'

'Don't you?'

'It would make more sense, considering the practicalities of holding up the body while they forced the nails through the flesh.'

I leant into the corpse. 'Did forensics find anything on the wrists and ankles of the other victims?'

'You mean apart from the nails and the blood?'

'Yes.' I examined the space on either side of the feet. 'It looks like something else was attached to the wall and then removed.'

She peered into the same spot. 'I'm not sure if they checked the walls, but I'll ask.'

Sara left to find a forensic officer. It allowed Coe to slide up to me, smelling of cheap aftershave and yesterday's pizza.

'Have you been inside this house before, Walker?'

'This is my first time.' I peered into the darkness that was his eyes. 'Though I guess you don't believe that?'

'You're keeping something from us, Walker, I know it. Sara might think you're a lovable goon, but I know better.' Coe moved closer to me. 'My contacts in the Met told me all about you, Frank, about your arrogance and how it pushed you over the edge.' He was near enough I could have wrung his neck. 'Then you ran home to your old man, and crime followed you there.' His grin added to my irritation. 'How is your brother, by the way?'

I ignored the question. 'I don't need to lie to you or anyone about this, Coe.'

He shook his head. 'The crucial part of any lie is that it must be believable. Not necessarily by everyone but by enough to create a margin of doubt, however small. It also helps if the lie feeds into the audience's weakness by telling them what they want to hear. Perhaps you're lying to yourself and don't even know it.'

He was looking for an argument, but I didn't give it to him.

'You've seen all four bodies at the crime scenes, Coe, so what do you think the connection is?'

'Apart from you?'

I sighed. 'If you put your fingers in your ears, they'd meet in the middle.'

He started another round of accusations against me. 'Did you make Cash swallow that bag with your name inside it before you killed him so you could insert yourself into the investigation?'

My temperature increased as the blood boiled under my skin.

'How did someone as stupid as you get to be the Senior Investigating Officer on this case, Coe? If I were a cynic, I might think somebody wants you here to mess the whole thing up.'

I watched him raise his hand, waiting for the blow to come before Sara returned.

'Forensics will check the walls for foreign substances after removing the former assistant chief constable.'

I turned to her. 'What?'

'Yeah, this is Mark Blair, seventy-five-year-old former assistant chief constable for this county.'

'Christ,' I said.

'A high-ranking copper,' Coe said. 'I'll say this for you, Walker, you're ambitious. Did you ever cross paths with Blair while at the Met?'

Had I? I couldn't tell anything from his face since the pain had distorted it so much.

'I'm not sure.'

The forensic team arrived to remove the body, so the three of us stepped away. I was hoping Coe would bugger off to do his job, but he lingered around like an unpleasant smell that was even worse than the aroma in the room.

'Do you want to have a look through the house?' Sara said.

'Why not?' If nothing else, I wouldn't have to put up with Coe.

She took me upstairs first. 'Do you recognise Blair?'

'His wife wouldn't recognise him from that face, Sara, but no.'

She stopped me halfway up. 'Four male pensioners murdered in a ten-mile radius. All of them were retired, but we have a farmer, solicitor, journalist, and high-ranking police officer. What does that say to you, Frank?'

'Not a lot, but Lydia thinks it might be class war.'

'What?'

'Yeah, I don't believe that either. Perhaps we should check this house first to see if anything can shed light on all of this.'

Sara kept quiet as we went through the bathroom and bedrooms, searching through clothes, linen baskets, and under the beds. All I saw was a life of luxury for a retired couple, but nothing that told me why this had happened or what it had to do with me. We returned downstairs together.

'I'll take the back room while you check the library,' Sara said as Coe eyed us from the living room doorway.

The library contained hundreds of magazines and books, though it appeared they hadn't been disturbed for several years. I wiped the dust from copies of *Home and Gardens* and *The New Scientist*, resisting the urge to sneeze. My legs ached, so I sat on the nearest sofa, glancing at the replica Klimt paintings on the wall. Between them was a framed copy of *The Scream*, the image perfectly replicating the contents of my head.

There had to be a reason why Coe was harassing me so much beyond his blatant incompetence. Was he another ghost from my youth, someone holding a grudge against me for all these years? Could he even be the one who placed my name at the previous murder scene? The whole thing seemed as ridiculous as Coe's claims against me.

I shook the idea from my head and got up to look at the books. I was glancing through them when I heard a shout from the living room. When I returned, the victim had been removed from the wall and laid onto a stretcher. I knew a complete medical examination of the body wouldn't happen until they got it to the mortuary for the post-mortem. Still, one officer dressed head to toe in a protective white overall was peering into Blair's eviscerated chest.

'The heart's missing,' he said.

'Fuck!' DCI Coe breathed down my neck.

This was new. They had removed no organs from the other three victims. As I contemplated what it meant, Sara called for me.

'Walker, come to the kitchen.'

I left Coe shaking his head, knowing there weren't many brain cells moving around inside. Other SOCOs passed me into the living room as I went to Sara. She was staring into the fridge when I got there.

'The former assistant chief constable has no heart,' I said.

Darkness consumed her face as she looked at me. 'I know where it is.'

I moved to her side and peered at the flickering light, discovering the missing organ.

I took a deep breath. 'Do you want me to remove it?'

Sara looked at me as if I'd asked her if she wanted me to make her a sandwich. Then she reached into her pocket and got a clear plastic evidence pouch.

'Are you sure your heart is in it, Frank?'

I grabbed the plastic and held it open for her. She

dropped the organ in the bag, surprising me with her flippancy until I remembered all the violent crime scenes I'd attended. If you didn't keep a sense of humour – even a dark one – the job would drive you insane, eventually.

I peered into the fridge, seeing if there were more human organs, when I noticed what the heart had rested on. Sara handed the evidence bag to a SOCO as I grasped the paper and unfolded it.

Then it was my turn to swear.

'Fucking hell!'

It was printed from a news website and was the worst headline I'd ever seen. Sara stood behind me and read it out.

'Disgraced Met copper sacked for discovering where serial killer Christopher Matthews buried his victims.' She held another evidence bag open for the paper and stared at me. 'Do you still think these murders are nothing to do with you, Frank?'

13 HEART OF GLASS

I stood in the kitchen, my bones feeling like I was in the freezer. Sara was speaking to Coe in the living room. I couldn't hear the words, but his glee was unmistakable. SOCOs came in to process the fridge; my eyes focused on where the heart had sat on the paper. Another bloodied piece of evidence with my name on it.

How could I continue to say these crimes had nothing to do with me?

Yet, there was no mention of me at the first crime scenes. So why these last two?

I left the officers to their work, slipping out of the house to find Lydia sitting on the wall opposite. She put her phone away as I approached her.

'The internet is going wild about this latest murder,' she said.

The wind whistled around my head, sending chills down my spine.

'Saying what?'

'Serial Killer Stalks The North is the gist of it.' She glanced over my shoulder. 'How bad was it in there?'

'Bad,' I said. There was no point telling her the gruesome details of the missing heart. Or of my connection to it.

She jumped off the wall. 'Let's go back to my place for a drink.'

'Frank's coming to the station,' Sara said as she joined us.

I turned to her. 'Why?'

'You know why, Frank.' She nodded at Coe, who was staring at me from across the road. 'I talked him out of arresting you here and now.'

'Arresting him for what?' Lydia said.

I puffed out my cheeks and told her what we'd found in the fridge. Then I spoke to Sara.

'Am I under suspicion of any crime?'

She shook her head. 'No. Regardless of Coe's antipathy to you, we have nothing to implicate you in these murders, but we would like a formal statement from you.'

I knew she was right and didn't need to make things harder for her. Plus, I wouldn't give Coe any more ammunition to fuel his warped theories about me.

'Okay, Sara. I'll join you in a second.'

I grabbed Lydia, standing beside me, open-mouthed, and led her back to the car.

She wriggled from my grasp. 'Your name, under the latest victim's heart, was in the fridge?'

My mouth felt like a desert, and I was desperate for something alcoholic.

'Yeah. How freaky is that?'

'You'll call me when you arrive home?' she said.

I watched her get into the car. 'I promise.'

She left, and I joined Sara in the back of a police car.

It was a silent drive to the station. When we arrived, Sara mentioned it wouldn't be a formal interview – I was only helping them with their enquiries – but if I wanted a lawyer, she'd understand. I didn't take up her offer of legal representation.

Then Coe had a grand old time when he and Sara got me into an interview room.

'That's two victims out of four connected to you now, Walker.' On the table between us was evidence wrapped in plastic. 'And I bet if we dig deeper into the first murders, we'll discover a connection to you there.'

'Your officers have already done that,' I said, 'and there's no link to me at either of them.'

He held up the evidence bag with the paper from the fridge and my name in large capital letters gazing back at me.

'So, how do you explain this?'

'Maybe the killer is working their way up to me,' I said without believing it.

However, perhaps it was true. I'd made plenty of enemies during my time at the Met, and it could be an extravagant manner of getting back at me.

Coe shook his head, and I imagined he thought this case might be his making, a chance to get away from the parochial northeast and into a better job in one of the country's bigger cities like Leeds or Manchester. Then, if he got lucky and played his cards right, it could only be a few short years before he was working in London. Maybe even with some of my former colleagues.

Or this might go all to crap, and he'd police flocks of sheep in the Outer Hebrides.

'It's more than that, Walker, and I think you know it.'

I took a sip of the coffee Sara had brought me.

'Are you still spouting that nonsense about me wanting to be involved in the search for another serial killer so I could be in the limelight? Or, something equally unlikely, I'm doing this to get my job back with the Met?'

He only smiled. The conversation wasn't being recorded, so he could have spouted any old guff at me, but I thought he couldn't believe that fantasy he'd dreamt about me.

So why did he say it?

Sara spoke. 'We now have confirmation of a definite connection between you and the last two victims, Frank.' I didn't reply. 'The only link we have between the murders of David Cash and Mark Blair is you.'

I crossed my arms. 'That's not true, DI Rose. The method of the crimes, the nailing of the bodies in an upside-down crucifix, connects them. Anybody could have left the printed article about my last case at the Met in that fridge. You can ask Mrs Blair about it when she wakes up in the hospital.'

If she woke. The trauma of what had happened to her husband must have affected her body and mind.

Sara peered straight into my eyes. 'Frank, you know from your considerable experience with crimes like this – with perpetrators like this – that if they leave messages for the police, there's usually a reason. Printing your name and then sealing it into a clear plastic bag before forcing the third victim, David Cash, to swallow it was not a random act of madness. The killer, or killers, intended us to find it. It's the same with the article about you we found underneath Mark Blair's heart in the fridge. They left it with the heart for us to discover. We're trying to understand what this all means and its connection to you.'

I looked past her to where Coe sat, glaring at me. I needed to understand it as well.

'Have you called in the National Crime Agency yet?'

The NCA had analysts who dealt with these sorts of crimes, creating profiles of serial killers and other violent offenders.

He continued to glare. 'We don't need any FBI wannabees interfering with this case, Walker. It won't be long before we have it solved.'

The FBI dig was because that's how most of the media viewed the NCA. So if he wasn't asking for their help, that decision hadn't come from him but from somebody higher up, possibly the Chief Constable.

But why? It could only benefit the investigation, having experienced analysts looking at the evidence. Was it to do with the last victim, Mark Blair, the former assistant chief constable?

'Well, I'll keep telling you this until I'm blue in the face – I don't know why the killers left my name at the last two crime scenes.'

Sara crossed her arms. 'You've met none of the victims before?'

She knew I hadn't, but I understood why she had to ask again.

'You know I only returned here a few months ago, Inspector Rose. And that was my first visit back in over twenty-five years.'

Coe put the bloodied paper in the bag on the table. Then he placed photographs of four retired men in front of me: images of them as they were before the crucifixions.

'What about when you lived here as a teenager, Frank? Did you know any of the victims then?'

I peered at the photos. The names and their ages at the time of death were printed on them: Robert Baker, 80; Harold Burke, 77; David Cash, 75; and Mark Blair, 75. A farmer, a solicitor, a journalist, and a copper in their former lives. A high-ranking copper.

So what connected them all?

Apart from being crucified upside down.

'I'm not sure what you've heard about me, Coe, but I didn't hang around with blokes in their forties or fifties when I was a teenager.'

He grinned at me. 'Of course, when you were a young lad, you were knocking about with the likes of Tony Thompson, one of Whiteport's more popular gangsters.'

'What Thompson did after I left is nothing to do with me.' I glanced at the pictures of the dead men. 'Are you sure there are no other links between these people?'

'We've checked online,' Sara said, 'but the records only go back so far. If the victims knew each other in their younger days, we haven't found the evidence yet.'

'Have you asked their families?' I said.

'Burke and Cash are widowers with no children. Baker's wife divorced him thirty years ago and passed away last year. Blair's daughter lives in Spain, and, as you know, his wife is currently unconscious in the hospital.'

I picked up Baker's photo, remembering all those framed pictures on the wall in his house. I didn't recall seeing a wife or any women in them.

'Have you looked into how the wives died?'

Coe laughed at me. 'Are you gasping at straws now, Walker?'

'Grasping,' I said. 'The expression is grasping at straws, and no, I'm not. Every avenue is worth exploring, don't you think?'

'We have studied them,' Sara said. 'Two were from heart attacks; the other was a hit and run.'

'Was the driver caught?'

'No.'

I rubbed my chin as my stomach growled. The four had to be connected, yet we couldn't see it.

'Let me get this clear, Walker,' Coe said. 'Are you saying you never knew or contacted any of the victims when you were younger and living in Whiteport?'

I took a deep breath. 'I wish this was on tape so I could say on record how much of an idiot you are, Coe. Instead, I'll repeat myself – I don't know and have met none of the four victims of the so-called Crucifix Murderer.' My stomach rumbled again, and I got up. 'So if there are no more questions, I'm going home.'

I left the room before he could protest. Or before he could say something even more stupid like I was off to the hospital to silence the comatose Mrs Blair.

Sara stopped me before I exited the station.

'You're connected to this, Frank, whether or not you like it.'

I laughed at her. 'Why would I like it?'

She shrugged. 'You know what I mean.' She leaned in closer so none of the prying eyes could hear. 'And what you told Coe isn't strictly true.'

'What does that mean?'

'You said you'd met none of the victims when you were younger and living here, but you can't be sure about that since it was so long ago.'

'Sara, I know you mean well, but come on. A farmer, a solicitor, a journalist and a copper: how would a teenage me get to meet people like that?'

I didn't wait for an answer, stepping into the street as my stomach grumbled again. The thought of food filled my head as I left the police station behind, but no matter what culinary delicacy I focused on, I soon replaced it with the image of that heart sitting in the fridge.

And of the paper underneath it.

14   HIS LATEST FLAME

Lydia was waiting for me when I left the police station. And so were dozens of people yelling at me and taking photos. I raised one arm to cover my face like a guilty person staggering out of court. I ignored the questions and stumbled into Lydia's car.

'I thought you'd gone home.'

She started the engine and switched the radio on to drown out the sounds of those knocking on the window.

'I knew you'd need a lift, Frank.'

Agitated faces scrutinised me through the glass, their lips moving at a thousand miles a second, their eyes peering deep into mine. Was this only a taster of what was to come once my face and name were pasted across the media next to the words Crucifix Killer?

Straight To Hell, by The Clash, blared out of the speakers as the crowd thrust their cameras and phones towards us as Lydia drove away.

'I need more than that.' My stomach rumbled again. 'I'm starving.' I watched the police station disappear in the mirror behind us. 'Do you have food at your place?'

'Of course. Do you want to stay at mine tonight and avoid the paparazzi loitering around your house?'

'Christ, I hadn't even thought about that. So you think they have my name already?'

She shrugged. 'Some copper will leak it, eventually.'

Lydia was right, but I'd have to go home at some point. Still, there was no rush now, and I didn't fancy being on my own in that house again.

'Okay, I'll let you cook me a meal. I assume you have booze as well?'

She laughed as Kate Bush started running up that hill again.

'So, Frank, what happened at the cop shop?'

I told her about Coe's continued obsession with me. 'I don't think he likes me.'

She tried to lighten the mood. 'How could anyone not like you, Walker?'

I peered at the flickering streetlights passing us by. 'Somebody likes me enough to leave my name after crucifying two people.'

Lydia shook her head. 'I still can't believe the killers removed his heart, put it in the fridge, and underneath it was an article about you and the serial killer Christopher Matthews.'

'That's about the gist of it.'

'That's more than a gist, Frank.'

'Somebody is setting me up.' It was the only reason I could think for my name being left at the murder scenes.

'Why?' she said.

I had no reply, letting her drive and ignoring my growing hunger. We didn't speak again until we were in her flat and she'd made us both coffee. The wine was calling to me, but I needed food before I could touch any alcohol.

We'd got fish and chips from a nearby place and ate them straight from the paper. I'd also avoided watching the TV and browsing the internet for fear of seeing my mug on either. I had no desire to talk about what had happened, but Lydia was keen.

'Somebody is definitely trying to tell you something, Frank.'

'I know, but what?'

She dropped three sugars into her drink. 'There must be a reason that news article about Matthews was there.' The coffee aroma engulfed my senses. 'Why leave that particular one at the scene.'

I shrugged. 'Well, it's the only case I'm famous for – or infamous. And it was in the fridge because it was with the heart.'

'I guess, but....' She scratched at her arm. 'It's more than highlighting your name again; it has to be. A heart and a fridge.'

'You're overthinking this.'

'I'm not. A heart and a fridge.' She drank the coffee, grimaced, and then dropped two more sugars into it. 'It must be connected to what happened between you and Matthews. He hasn't escaped, has he?'

A shudder ran down my spine. 'It would have been all over the news if he had.'

'What about relatives? Does he have any? Or could there be somebody who loved him who now wants to hurt you?'

'He's an only child, and his parents died years ago. I'm unsure about loved ones seeking revenge, but anything is possible.'

'Perhaps you should pay him a visit?'

I nearly choked on a chip. 'What?'

'You know, like Clarice and Hannibal Lecter. See if you can get an insight into this crucifix serial killer by talking to the one you helped put behind bars.'

I shook my head. 'This isn't the movies, Lydia.'

She grinned at me. 'You got that right, Frank. Nobody would ever accuse you of having movie-star good looks.'

I raised my coffee to her. 'Cheers.'

'Still, you have a doctor and a multi-millionaire sniffing around you.'

'For a modern lady, you come out with some terrible language.'

Her laughter hurt my ears. 'That's the first time anybody has accused me of being a lady. And, for an old man, you're a bit of a prude. But I digress – do you prefer the worthy woman or the wealthy one?'

'Lydia, I've too much on my mind to consider dating anyone.' And the thought terrified me.

'Don't be daft, Walker. This is the perfect time for you to wine and dine some lucky person. You need a distraction from the other stuff, wouldn't you say?'

I settled into the sofa and stared at her. The fish and chips had taken residency in my gut, making my brain sluggish, but perhaps she was right.

'I can't ask Dr Carlisle for a date while my dad's still in the hospital. It wouldn't seem appropriate.'

She laughed at me. 'That's a wonderful excuse for dating a millionaire. So give the lovely Eva a call before you bottle out of it. Or before we find you upside down and crucified.'

'Thanks for that, but I don't have her number.'

'Well, it's a good job I do.'

She passed her phone across the table to me. On the screen was Eva Cross's number.

'When did you get this?'

'Jeez, Frank, you're sometimes pretty slow on the uptake for a former detective. When do you think I got it?'

'At the party the other night?'

She clapped her hands. 'Bingo for Bonzo.'

I added the number to my mobile contacts. Then I just stared at it.

'I should probably wait until my dad gets out of the hospital.'

'Stop putting it off, Frank.'

I stood, grabbing the wine and two glasses, pouring a large measure for us. The smell rushed up my nose and tickled my senses.

'What if she's seen the news, and I'm all over it?'

Lydia retrieved her phone and peered at the screen. 'There's no mention of you on any of the main websites or the local ones. They're obsessed with the victim since he was a former high-ranking copper, speculating it might be a revenge killing. All the low-life sites focus on the Crucifix Killer and theorise that the murders must have a religious connection.'

'I'm unsure if I should ask Eva on a date, not right now.'

She flicked at the screen on her phone. 'Would you like me to speak to her for you?'

Electricity surged through my chest and grasped at my heart. 'No, I'll do it.'

I took a deep breath, puffed out my cheeks and called the number. Part of me hoped there would be no answer or I'd reach the machine, but she answered after three rings.

'Hello.'

Even that one word down the line made my chest flutter.

'Er, hello, Eva. It's Frank Walker.' I struggled with the words. 'I was wondering how you are.'

Lydia looked at me and stuck two fingers near her throat as if she was about to throw up.

'I'm fine, Frank. How is your father?'

'Oh, he's well, doing okay now. He's awake, but the docs will keep him in for a few more days to ensure he's recovered. So, that's why I'm calling, really, because I'm going to be on my own, and I wondered if you would like to go for a drink or something.'

I knew it sounded stupid as I was saying it. Lydia put her hands around her neck and pretended to choke herself.

At least, I guessed she was pretending.

'That would be great, Frank. When and where did you have in mind?'

I'd assumed she'd say no, so I hadn't given the rest any thought. Lydia typed like a dervish on her phone as I struggled for any coherence. Then she showed me the screen, and I replied to Eva.

'How about tomorrow at eight at the Italian restaurant near your community centre?'

'Fantastic,' Eva said. 'But it's not my centre, Frank. I've donated it to the people to commemorate the building that stood there for fifty years.'

'Well,' I said. 'That's another reason for us to celebrate.'

'That sounds great, but I've got one request.'

'Okay.' I waited for her to tell me to bring Lydia.

'You need to wear something casual, not a suit, t-shirt or shorts. Can you do that for me?'

I stared at Lydia, who had a hand over her mouth to control her laughter.

'Yeah, I think so. I have a personal stylist now.'

'Excellent. I'll see you tomorrow.'

I agreed and finished the call. Lydia was scrutinising me as if she was measuring up for a coffin.

'Do you have any decent clothes for a date with a rich woman, Walker?'

'You heard what she said?'

'You've got the volume turned up so high I think my neighbours probably heard the conversation.'

Then the fear hit me. 'What am I going to wear?'

Lydia rubbed at her chin. 'You know, I still have a few of Uncle Tony's clothes that might fit you, big as you are. And he was quite a snappy dresser. No suits, just smart casual.'

I stuck out my chest in protest. 'I'm not wearing anything of his.' The thought of wearing Tony Thompson's second-hand clobber made me cringe.

'Okay, keep your hair on. I'll have to take you to the shops then.'

'Great,' I said with no enthusiasm. 'I just love clothes shopping.'

Lydia nodded. 'We'll do it tomorrow afternoon, but I must visit somewhere first.' She grinned at me. 'And I think you should come with me. We could kill two birds with one stone, and you can do something you should have a long time ago.'

'Where do you have to go?'

Even as I asked, I guessed her answer.

'I'm off to the prison to visit Uncle Tony, so why don't you see your brother as well? Then we'll get your new clobber for tomorrow's hot date. What do you say?'

Going shopping with Lydia and visiting my brother in prison.

What could I say but yes?

Lydia placed breakfast in front of me, a bouquet of fried meat and hot beans massaging my taste buds.

'Are you trying to fatten me up?'

'You'll need a full stomach where you're going, Frank.'

I emptied the brown sauce over the sausage and bacon, keeping it away from the beans. Beans and brown sauce were for philistines.

'I've visited several prisons before, Lydia.'

She sat at the table as her cat jumped onto her lap. It gazed at me with barely disguised suspicion. Perhaps Coe had snuck into the flat to have a word with it.

'Of course, I'd forgotten you used to be a copper. How did that ever slip my mind?'

I ignored her sarcasm and glanced at the TV in the other room. Animated talking heads flickered on the screen, but with the sound down. I nodded towards it.

'You've watched some of that this morning?'

'I did while you were singing in the shower. You need a more modern repertoire than the Velvet Underground if you intend to serenade the lovely Eva Cross tonight. Or do you still have the hots for Dr Kitty Carlisle?'

Her digs at my so-called romantic life didn't affect me.

'I must ring the hospital before leaving for the prison to check on my father.'

'No problem, Frank.'

'So, was there anything on the TV about me?'

'Not so far, but you are on the internet.' She showed me her phone, the screen set on the local news website, and a blurred photo of me in her car outside the police station.

'Is it all bad?'

She shrugged. 'It's pretty neutral. It mentions you being seen at the last crime scene and repeats the highlights of your career at the Met, but there's no mention of the coppers finding your name with the victims of the Crucifix Killer.'

I cringed as I ate a slice of crispy bacon. 'The media are sticking with that name, then?'

'It looks like it.' The sparkle had vanished from her eyes, and I guessed she was keeping something from me.

'What is it, Lydia?'

The cat, Fudge, purred in her lap as she stroked its head.

'Some people online are putting your appearance at the last murder scene down to the desperation of the police.'

'Coe's desperate, I'll give you that, but what do you mean?'

'With your success with Matthews and the local plod clueless in identifying the Crucifix Killer, or killers, theories are doing the rounds that Detective Chief Inspector Coe asked for your help on this case.'

I nearly spat coffee all over the cat.

'God, I'd love to have seen Coe's face when he read that.'

'Well, it's not entirely untrue, is it? Sara wanted you to look at the crime scenes to see if anything jumped out at you.'

I wondered why Sara hadn't contacted me after the drama at the police station. Was that Coe's doing, or did even she believe I was involved in these murders?

The beans warmed my throat as I changed the conversation.

'How often have you visited Uncle Tony in prison?'

She jerked her legs to the side, and the cat jumped to the floor, glaring at me as it wandered into the living room.

'I go every week. No matter what he did, he's still family.'

'You must have some riveting conversations with him.'

Lydia got up. 'What will you say to your brother when you see him?'

Yes, what was I going to talk to Tommy about? There was only one thing we had in common.

'I'll tell him about the old man's failing health.'

'So you won't chat about why he's inside?'

I stood and stretched my arms, flexing my fingers and picturing the damage I'd done to Tommy's hand over thirty years ago. I'd always told myself it was an accident, chopping off the tops of his fingers with a kitchen knife while attempting to move the blade quickly between his fingers, but perhaps I'd meant it on purpose as he believed.

'If he wants to talk about that, we will.' Then something important came to me. 'I can't go now – I didn't contact the authorities to book a visit.' Contrary to popular belief, you couldn't just walk into a correctional facility without permission.

Lydia smiled at me. 'Don't worry, Frank; I did that for you.'

My legs froze to the spot as I stared at her. 'We only decided last night I was going to the prison today.'

'I told you, I've visited Uncle Tony every week. So, I've been booking times for you as well, just in case you joined me.'

'And you cancelled them when I didn't?'

'All apart from today.'

I admired her ingenuity and wondered if she knew me better than I knew myself. I'd tried not to think of Tommy since his sentence, but I understood I'd have to see him at some point. And with the old man's deteriorating health, it would always be sooner rather than later. I had no great desire to speak to my older brother, but he was entitled to know what was happening to our father.

'How is Tony adjusting to prison life?'

'He's getting used to it.'

I could tell from how she narrowed her eyes that she didn't want to talk about him. And I didn't blame her. She was loyal to the only family she had, but Thompson had lied to her, leading to innocent people suffering.

'We might as well be off, then.'

'After the visit, we'll buy you some new clothes for your big date tonight, Frank.'

I grimaced at her, wondering what would be worse: visiting my brother in jail or shopping with Lydia.

FORTY MINUTES LATER, we were striding through the gates of the local prison. Once the staff had checked our IDs, we went through a security process similar to what you get at an airport. There were dogs to sniff out drugs, one of which had a particular interest in Lydia, but that must have been because they could smell the cat on her. Then a guard led us into the visiting room. This was a large area with tables and chairs where other visitors waited to see prisoners. I took a seat far from Lydia, not wanting to be near Tony Thompson. Security scrutinised everyone, but they were far enough away to have a private conversation without worrying they were spying on you.

Then the inmates filtered in. I noticed that the younger ones, guys in their late teens and early twenties, had female visitors their age. Blokes in their late twenties and early thirties had family, usually a mother figure with a young child waiting for them. The silence transformed into excited chatter quickly as the room soon filled with every emotion imaginable - joy, tears, shame, anger, and everything in between.

There were no mirrors in the room. I assumed this was because the authorities didn't want the inmates peering at themselves when they were deprived of their liberty. Or perhaps it was to prevent them from breaking the glass to use as weapons against others or themselves. If visitors needed to use the bathroom, they had to wait for a guard to open the door.

Tony Thompson and my brother were the last to enter, smiling at each other as if they were walking into a nightclub. As they separated and Tommy saw me, I wondered how close they were. Perhaps they'd reminisced about the old days in Whiteport while exercising in the gym, or they'd swapped stories of their teenage years while slopping the prison gruel into their gobs.

My brother grinned as he sat opposite me.

'When the screws told me I had a visitor, I assumed it

must be Santa Claus. But, of course, that was more believable than thinking it would be you, Frank.'

I turned my hands into fists under the table. 'I'm not here by choice.'

He crossed his arms. 'So why are you here, little brother?'

I took a deep breath. 'Dad's not well, Tommy.'

My brother's laugh was loud enough to turn heads in the room.

'The old man? That's why you're here?'

'I thought you should know.'

He put his hands on the table, and I stared at the damage I'd done to him so many years ago.

'He's ninety-three, Frank; he's always going to be ill.'

I resisted the urge to get up and leave. I'd told him the news about our father, so my responsibility was over.

'I'll pass on your good words when I see him in hospital, Tommy.'

He flexed the remaining fingers on his hand. 'There's something you could do for me.'

What a surprise. 'Such as?'

He glanced at the prison staff before leaning closer to me.

'It's violent and dangerous in here, Frank. I've already had inmates trying to stab me.' The fear in his eyes was real. 'I don't know how long I can stay safe. So I need your help.'

'Why should I help you?'

He moved back into his seat. 'Because you're my brother. Think of all the times I protected you when we were kids.'

I thought of that. 'You did nothing for me, Tommy. Your memory must be on the way out like the old man's.'

He shook his head. 'You owe me, Frank.' He held up his damaged hand. 'You owe me for this.'

'Any debt I had to you was extinguished when you tried to kill me.'

He smiled at me. 'That was just a misunderstanding. You shouldn't hold grudges because of that. So, will you use your police contacts to get me into a different prison?'

'You haven't been paying attention, Tommy; I don't have any friends left in the force.'

His face darkened as he peered at me.

'I read about you in the news today, Frank. The local pigs need you to help them solve some serial killer case. You can use that influence to have me moved out of here.'

'Have you made friends in here, Tommy?'

He puffed out his cheeks. 'Haven't you been paying attention? People are trying to kill me, and the screws are letting them. I must get out as soon as possible, preferably to one of those open prisons.'

I examined his face, recognising his fear but unconcerned for him. He'd stopped being my brother long ago, and his attempt to murder me had erased any lingering brotherly connection I might have had.

'Have you heard any rumours in here about the crucifix murders, Tommy?'

He scrunched up his eyes. 'If I have, will you help me?'

'Tell me what you know.'

He glanced at the closest prison guard. 'Only if you promise to help me.'

I sat there silently, wondering if he was about to lie to me again. Then I got up, ready to leave.

'Enjoy your life, Tommy. I won't be returning.'

He jerked out of his seat and grabbed my arm. The guard moved just as quick, marching towards us.

'Release him, Walker,' he shouted.

Everybody looked at us, including Lydia. I shook my brother off me.

'Don't go, Frank.'

His pleading irritated the rock in my heart, but I left him anyway, striding towards the exit.

'I'll wait for you outside, Lydia.'

As I exited, I thought I heard my brother crying.

16 ANOTHER GIRL, ANOTHER PLANET

Going shopping for clothes with Lydia proved less painful than visiting my brother. After splashing out on a new suit, we stopped to see my father at the hospital. He'd improved a little, and Dr Carlisle said he'd be able to come home as soon as they organised a system of care with the local social services.

'As long as that's what you want, Frank,' she said to me.

I still wasn't sure what the best thing for the old man was, but I was happy to take her advice.

'Let's give it a few weeks' trial, Kitty, and see how it goes.'

We agreed on that, and I left the hospital as my father flirted with a nurse seventy years younger than him. She didn't appear too bothered about it, but I felt guilty for heading home to get ready for a date with Eva Cross while still having feelings for Kitty.

Lydia must have read my mind as I got into the car.

'You're going out for a meal and a few drinks, Frank; you're not getting married.'

'Have you ever been attracted to more than one person simultaneously?' I asked her.

She laughed as she drove out of the hospital.

'Jesus, Walker, everybody in the world has felt like that at some point.' She shook her head at me. 'How old are you?'

'Forty-five.'

'So you're a bloke rushing towards fifty, and this is the first time it's happened to you?'

'Hey, let's have less talk of me rushing towards fifty.'

She grinned. 'Okay. You're turning into a frustrated teenager, anyway.'

I scratched at the back of my neck. 'I feel like one.' But at least it was keeping my mind off the crucifixion murders. 'I hope I don't look like an idiot in that new suit.'

'You should have bought the purple one, as I said.'

'Yes, Lydia, I'm sure Eva would be very impressed with me turning up tonight dressed as the Joker.'

'Well, if you make her laugh, you'll capture her heart.'

I didn't want to think about capturing hearts as all it did was make my picture what we'd discovered in that fridge.

'What will you do while I'm at the restaurant?'

'Don't worry about me, Frank. Fudge and I will watch something on Netflix. I've heard so many good things about this German show called *Dark*.' She glanced at me as she drove. 'Or do you want me out of the flat so you can entertain Eva after your meal?'

'I'm not thinking that far ahead.' There were four hours to go, and I felt as nervous as a teenager preparing for their first date.

'You're out of practice, Walker. Would you like me to give you tips on what the modern woman is looking for in a man?'

The laughter came out of me like smoke from a bellow.

'I'm twice your age, and you'll give me romantic advice?'

'Well, you haven't had much luck with the ladies, have you?'

'I was married for five years.'

'Yes, you were married – past tense. And things have moved on since then. You need to understand the modern woman's needs, Frank; otherwise, you'll never be able to fulfil them.'

I shook my head. 'I'd rather spend an afternoon with DCI Coe than get sex advice from you, Lydia.'

She pulled a face at me. 'Don't be so disgusting. I'm talking about emotional and intellectual needs, not the physical. You can make that up as you go along.'

'I'd sooner not talk about any of this.'

She shook her head. 'Okay, Frank, have it your way, but don't come crying to me when it all goes horribly wrong.'

That was the last she said about it on the drive to her flat. When we got back, she took the cat for a walk – I still couldn't get over seeing the moggy on a lead – while I spent the time scouring the news and the internet for any updates on the crucifix murders. Speculation was rife with several theories, but most focused on a religious connection between the victims, though nobody had found one yet.

Thankfully, my name featured little in the theories, apart from those assuming the police had brought me in as a "consultant" on serial killers. I laughed off those comments until I discovered a link that took me to a Reddit forum about me. I hadn't known such a thing existed and was reluctant to delve into it, but I couldn't help myself.

I shouldn't have.

Half of what I read was from posters questioning my

honesty as a police officer: sample quote – "I bet Walker was working with Matthews, so they'll release a book together about the crimes. It's all about the money for coppers like him. And everyone knows how corrupt the Met is."

The poster was anonymous, but I imagined it might have come from DCI Coe's home computer.

Even the posts praising me made my spine twitch: "He did the right thing in tricking Matthews into spilling the beans about where the bodies were, but I wish he'd strangled the bastard afterwards."

Most of the comments were from the time of the Matthews investigation, but someone had bumped several to the top of the forum in the last twenty-four hours. Now, the posters focused on my involvement in the latest murders.

"The coppers need Walker to solve the case."

"He knows something they don't."

"My cousin works at the police station, and she says they've called Walker in on the recommendation of a clairvoyant."

That one made me laugh. But the others didn't.

"I heard the pigs think Walker is the Crucifix Killer, getting back at those who hurt him when he was a kid."

"The killer wrote Walker's name on the walls in blood, as the Manson Family did with Helter Skelter."

After that, I stopped reading, reaching for my phone and the Beatles playlist. I turned the Bluetooth on and linked it to Lydia's speakers. I listened to John Lennon telling me to turn off my mind and did just that.

LYDIA STOOD over me when I woke.

'Are you ill, Frank?'

I rubbed the sleep from my eyes. 'What time is it?'

'Seven-thirty. You better get a move on for your hot date.'

I lurched to my feet. 'The restaurant is nearby.'

'Yeah, but you smell terrible. You need a wash before putting on that suit.'

She was right, so I took a quick shower and slipped into my new clobber. It felt tight around my arms, and I hoped it didn't make me resemble a squashed pig.

Lydia grinned at me. 'You look fantastic, Walker. If I was twenty years older, drunk and desperate, even I could take a shine to you.' The cat was on the table next to her, peering at me as if I was the trash Lydia had forgotten to throw out. 'Are you sure you don't need me to stay somewhere else tonight so you can have the flat to yourself?'

I shook my head. 'It's only food and drink between two people getting to know each other. I don't want anything else.'

At least for now. I had to straighten my life out before engaging in romantic entanglements.

Lydia stepped forward and touched my arm. 'Is your body failing you, Walker? Would you like me to get you some special pills from the internet?'

I pulled away from her as she burst out laughing.

'Don't wait up for me,' I said as I left.

Outside, peering across the dark and into the ocean, I let the cool breeze push me towards the restaurant, knowing I'd arrive on time.

Eva was waiting when I got there, sitting at a table near the window so we'd have a sea view for the date.

Was it a date? I couldn't remember the last time I'd had one.

She stood as I walked over, looking magnificent in dark trousers, a light top, and a green jacket that could have graced the latest issue of *Vogue* magazine.

'I like a punctual man, Frank.'

We sat opposite each other, the server standing between us before we could speak. Eva ordered a bottle of white wine while I admired her and the surroundings. Then I remembered her saying she hadn't touched a drop of alcohol in twenty years.

'You're drinking booze?'

Her smile sent a shiver along my neck.

'No, that's for you. I'll stick to water for now.'

An entire bottle of wine for me. Did she think I was an alcoholic?

'I'm sorry about the other day, Eva, having to leave you so abruptly.'

She sipped at her water as my drink arrived. 'Oh, I understand completely, Frank. Even when you're retired, something from your old life is always grasping for you to return.'

I let the alcohol chill my throat before speaking. 'You never had the opportunity to tell me about your time in Australia.'

'We've got all night for that.' She handed me a menu. 'Let's order our food first.'

I settled for a spaghetti Bolognese while she picked a seafood pasta dish. It was terrific, helped by me washing down half a bottle of wine while we talked.

'You lived in Sydney?' I said as the alcohol created a warm fuzz inside my head.

Eva smiled at me. 'Have you been checking up on me online, Frank?'

I returned her smile. 'Only a little.'

'That's only fair since I did the same with you.'

My knees trembled as I peered at the glint in those soft blue eyes, and I remembered that Reddit forum about me.

'You did that and still agreed to meet me?'

She laughed. 'Perhaps I like a bit of mystery and intrigue in my life – and you appear to have plenty of that right now.'

I dropped an ice cube into my glass of wine to water it down.

'You've seen today's news?'

'About you? I didn't have to since Cynthia and Alison Holgate called to give me the gory details. However, they seem to believe me associating with you might be bad for the community centre.' She finished her water, and I wished I'd kept away from the wine. 'What do you think?'

'Well, maybe you could add me to the group of local celebrities to promote the venue.'

I was only half-joking.

Eva continued laughing. 'This wasn't what I expected when leaving Australia.'

I didn't want to mention her husband's death, but was curious why she'd gone to live abroad.

'Was it a culture shock coming back here?'

She shrugged. 'I suppose so. I left this town on my sixteenth birthday, working in Berwick as a chambermaid in a hotel. Two years later, I was living in Edinburgh, which lasted until I was twenty-one, and I headed to Australia.' She gazed out of the window at the darkness of the sea. 'The weather was a vast improvement, but the country seemed three decades behind Britain. I'd met Peter within six months, and even though he was concerned about the ten-year age difference between us, I wasn't.'

'And you built your empire together?'

'Peter had an inheritance with no head for business. But I did, and I knew how the hotel chains worked, so that's where we started, with a single location in Sydney.' She held up her hands. 'And the rest, as they say, is history.'

'Well, I'm sure the residents of Billsdale are glad you've returned to bring something positive to the town.'

We continued to reminisce as we ate, with me telling her stories of my time at the Met and Eva recalling what it was like for a woman breaking down barriers in the business world in Australia.

I finished the last of the wine and toasted her success.

'Long may it continue,' I said as the words struggled over my lips.

'I think you might need some fresh air, Frank.'

I glanced beyond her and out the window, removing my credit card from my pocket.

'I know where there's plenty of that.'

'Put that away,' Eva said. 'Tonight's on me. You can pay next time.'

I didn't argue, happy to know there would be a next time.

Then we got up, and she led me into the night.

17 PICTURE THIS

The sea breeze hit me in the face like a punch to the gut. Eva grabbed me as I stumbled from the restaurant, her touch warming me instantly.

'Perhaps I should walk you back to Lydia's flat?'

I couldn't remember telling her I was staying there, but I must have. As I pulled her across the road towards the sea, I wrapped my arm in hers.

'In a minute,' I said. 'The wind is kicking my brain into action.'

Eva let me take her to the fishing boats docked near the wall. My belly was full, and I hadn't thought of the old man or the murders since I'd sat at that table with her. Now, those two things were rushing back into my mind, and I wanted to push them away again, even if it was only for a short while.

'What's wrong, Frank?' she said. 'You appear pained.'

I turned to her. 'I'm unsure if I want my father to return home if he can't look after himself anymore.'

She reached out to me, putting her hand on my arm.

Down below us, the waves crashed against the concrete while gulls swooned above our heads.

'I'm sure you'll do the right thing for you and him.'

Eva's certainty warmed my heart, but I wasn't as confident as her. I thought of the old man with his many health problems, my brother suffering in jail, and the crimes where the killers had left my name behind.

And none of it made me feel any better.

'I'm unsure if I've ever done the right thing, Eva.'

The booze played havoc with my brain, and I wished I'd stayed on the water. She pushed her body into mine, the scent of her perfume stealing its way through my skin, plunging deep into my heart and inflaming my senses.

'That can't be true, Frank. Think of all the good you did in the police and the people you must have helped.'

The tiny version of me running around aimlessly in my head tried to tell me she was right, that I had led a productive life, but the mixture of alcohol and self-doubt fought against her words. However, it didn't matter as I let myself sink into her embrace.

Then I saw the lights on at the new community centre.

'You might have burglars, Eva.'

She turned from me to stare at the building. 'The staff are preparing the memorial wall for the previous centre. We wanted to have it done for the official ceremony, but all the old photos and documents were in storage out of town. So if they're in there now, they must be putting the finishing touches on the display.'

It would have been easy to stay there, sinking deeper into her arms, but I needed a distraction from the thoughts bouncing inside my skull, a diversion from the images of my old man withering away, pinned to a wall and upside down.

'Why don't we have a peek inside? I'm always a sucker for a bit of history.'

She frowned before pulling me closer to her.

'I thought you weren't feeling well? Perhaps I should get you to bed.'

I was useless at reading potential romantic signals, but the sparkle in her eyes and the squeeze she gave my arm could only mean one thing.

Then panic swept through me.

I was out of practice and desperate not to fall into bed with her. Not that I didn't want to – God, did I want to – but the wine and my nerves were playing havoc with my body. I needed to sober up and calm down quickly. So, looking at some local history was a good way of diverting the chaos sweeping through me.

'I wouldn't mind seeing the display, Eva, if that's okay with you? My teenage years here are a bit of a blur, so the photos might kick start my memory.'

A smile replaced the frown. 'Okay, Frank, but let's make it a quick visit. I'll need the toilet soon. All that water is sloshing around inside me like a tidal wave.'

We got up together, her hand in mine sending warmth through my veins like a weeping volcano. She led me across the road and into the community centre. I expected to see somebody there, but it was empty. Eva went to the notice board covered in photographs.

'I'm glad they found some older pictures from the '70s and '80s.'

I glanced at my hand as my heart withered like a deflating balloon before turning to the photos. I peered at them, seeing those enjoying themselves in the old community centre, playing games, or participating in various activities: groups of teenagers gathered around pool tables;

women creating art or baking cakes; older folks playing bingo and drinking tea. The pictures were from thirty or forty years ago, but glancing at the people in them, without mobile phones or computers, devoid of the internet and social media, made them all seem as far away to me as the Victorian age or the industrial revolution.

After staring at them, they merged into an immense kaleidoscope of images. Then they transformed before my eyes into something completely different, into the family collection the old man kept in albums under his bed. My older sisters holding hands outside a primary school; my mother, unsmiling, cradling a baby; my brother with his arm around a grinning young woman; and finally, one of me as a child, sitting on the knee of a ventriloquist, gazing at the terrifying-looking dummy in his hand. Even now, in my hazy memory, the wooden doll seemed alive to me, with its huge grin ready to devour me.

I shook the family memories from my sight, returning to the display that celebrated the work Eva had done and the history of the community. I glanced over them before a photo in the top corner sparked my interest, and I moved closer to it. A middle-aged man stood smiling in the centre of a group of women holding cakes, a picture of a bloke I thought I'd seen recently in entirely different circumstances. I reached up and removed it from the board.

'Someone you know?' Eva said.

'I'm not sure.' I turned the photo over, reading the information on the back. 'June 20 1996.'

'That was the day the original centre closed. Does it mean anything to you that date?'

'Yeah, I was in Ibiza watching England lose to Germany on penalties in the European Championships.' Not that I cared too much about football, but that result ruined the holiday for the mates I was with.

Eva took the photo from me. 'It must have been traumatic for you to remember the exact date of the event.' She pointed at the picture. 'Do you know some of these people? It looks like a cake bake.'

'Can you hold it up for me?'

She did, and I used my phone to take a picture. Then I sent it to Sara with a message.

I know it's late, but do you recognise anybody here?

While waiting for a reply, I scrutinised the rest of the images on the board.

'These are the ones you said were in storage?'

Eva nodded. 'The twins organised the volunteers to bring them over. There are more boxes of them stored in the basement, hundreds, possibly thousands, along with other documents from the old community centre.'

'Can you show them to me?'

'This isn't how I expected our night to finish, Frank.'

I was wondering what she meant by that when Sara rang me.

'Where are you?'

'I'm at the community centre with Eva Cross. Do you know who she is?'

'Of course. Why are you there?'

I told her about the date. 'Eva was showing me the photos her staff took out of storage for the celebration, and I saw this one.'

'Have you looked through the others?'

'The ones on the boards, yes, but I don't recognise anyone.' I gazed at the photo again. 'Do you think that's a younger Robert Baker?'

'It definitely looks like him,' Sara said. 'What are you going to do now?'

'Eva is taking me to look at the rest of the photos and documents in the basement. Hopefully, there will be something useful in them.'

'Wait for me before you do anything. And don't go down into that basement until I get there.'

I laughed down the line. 'You believe the Crucifix Killer might be waiting for me?'

'Why not, Frank? I know you keep denying it, but I'm thinking this all about you.'

I peered at the old photo of Baker and the other volunteers from twenty-six years ago.

'No, Sara. This isn't about me. Somebody wants us all to think that, but it's only a distraction.'

'A distraction from what?'

'That's what I hope to discover in the basement.'

I ended the call before she could protest. Then I sent the photo in a message to Lydia.

See if you can find this image online or anything about the Billsdale Community Centre that stood in the same spot as the new one back in 1996.

She replied instantly.

Sure. Where are you?

I repeated what I'd told Sara. Then I went to Eva, standing in the corner, finishing her own phone call.

'I've checked with the custodian, and he said everything left over from the old centre is downstairs in several boxes. The documents haven't been stored in any order, so they're all mixed, photos with letters, memos and reports.'

'Was this custodian here in 1996?'

She shook her head. 'No. He took charge of them only five years ago. I believe it was connected to the church that used to run the centre in partnership with the council. There are stacks of boxes. Would you like to see them?'

I wanted nothing more than that but realised this wasn't the night she'd expected.

'I don't want to ruin our date.'

Eva narrowed her eyes at me. 'Is this a date?'

'Well....'

She touched my arm and laughed. 'I'm only joking, Frank.' She glanced at the photographs on the board. 'And I'm finding all of this rather exciting.'

'That's great. You better lead the way then.'

She let go of me and took me through a large door at the back of the room. Then it was down a narrow corridor to the top of the stairs. She flicked at a switch on the wall, but nothing happened.

'The lights aren't working.' She got her phone and turned the torch app on. 'I guess this will have to do. Do you have the same on your mobile?'

I looked for it as she opened the door.

'Here we go,' I said as I pointed the light ahead while remembering Sara had told me to wait for her.

But I couldn't do that. If that was Baker in the old photo, perhaps there were pictures of the other victims in the documents stored in the basement.

And maybe we finally had a lead in this case.

18   IN THE SHADOWS

We had to tread carefully in the gloom as we descended. Eva was just ahead of me, with our torches shining on half a dozen large cardboard boxes stacked against the far wall. Cobwebs were everywhere, and the place smelt as if it had been storing paint for the last thirty years, even though it was a new building. As we stepped into the basement, the air was icy, and I noticed papers scattered over the floor.

Eva shone her phone on the mess. 'It seems as if the staff were in a hurry when they searched for photos for the display upstairs.'

'I'm not so sure.' I moved nearer to the containers. 'These look like somebody threw them into the air without caring where they landed.'

I knelt to get a closer look, shining the torch over old bills, crumpled letters, and more photos. The concrete sent a chill into my leg as I used my free hand to rifle through the documents. Most of the paper was wrinkled and stained, smelling like it had been stored in a bin.

Eva moved next to me. 'Do you think there might be something useful in them?'

The light flickered as I passed the phone over the boxes.

'I'm not sure. It's probably better if I return tomorrow when we'll have more illumination.' My leg ached as I stood, and a chill covered my face. 'Can we get some heating in here as well, Eva?'

'I don't see why not.' She moved away, grabbing papers from the mess. 'Perhaps we should come back tomorrow.'

'Are you desperate for the toilet?'

I knew how she felt as my bladder was playing havoc with me. She didn't answer, and her light vanished. I turned to where I'd seen her last, swinging my mobile around. But she wasn't there. Had she left while I was looking through the papers?

Then I heard the groan from the corner. When I saw her lying on the floor, fear gripped my heart. I moved quickly, bending on one knee to see the bruise growing on her neck. When I put my phone down, I felt her breath on my palm and listened to her breathing. I got my hand under her head and lifted her towards me.

'Are you okay, Eva? Did you fall?'

Her eyes flickered open, her lips trembling as she tried to speak.

Then something struck me hard on my head.

My legs buckled, and I fell, missing Eva and hitting the ground next to her. I landed on my phone, and the lights went out. Pain rushed through me as I pushed my hands onto the floor. I tried to get up in the dark, touching Eva's arm as she groaned. But something thumped me again, across the face this time. Whatever it was cut deep, and the blood came immediately. The force knocked me back, and I hit a wall, agony speeding through my arm and shoulder. My lips sprang open as I struggled to breathe, finding dirt and dust invading my mouth. It was pitch black, but I could see something moving around: a large silver object.

A metal pipe.

The one that had already struck me twice after hitting Eva.

Now it flashed towards me again.

I reached up to grab it but missed, the steel crashing into my fingers and making me howl as it ripped nails and skin from me. The blood dripped down my cheek as I held my damaged hand. I twisted my neck to locate the attacker as the pipe returned, striking the wall this time. I jumped up and grasped into the dark, finding emptiness and hitting the ground near Eva. Then I thrust my arms up, clutching in vain for whoever was there. One hand flicked against something, but it wasn't enough to hold them. Then, the pipe hit my other cheek, tearing flesh from my face as I tumbled down into Eva.

I lay there as my eyes closed, waiting for another blow to crack my skull open.

But it didn't come.

There was deep breathing in the room, neither Eva's nor mine. I pushed my back into the wall, preparing to defend myself. The shadows flickered before me as I slumped into the floor. Cold concrete kissed my face as I pressed my skull into the dark.

The next thing I heard was Lydia's voice and a light shining on my face.

'Don't move them until the medics get here.'

That was Sara speaking.

Then I passed out.

I WAS LYING on a stretcher in the community centre lobby when I came round. A nuclear bomb had exploded inside my skull while a thousand suns shimmered over my eyes. I could taste blood in the back of my throat, and I wanted to throw up.

'Are you okay, Frank?'

That was Lydia again. I rubbed my head, blinked a dozen times and then stared into worried faces.

'What happened?' I said.

'Somebody attacked you in the basement.'

I jerked upright, and pain sped through my arm and shoulder before resting on my cheek.

'Eva?'

'She's fine. It looks like you got the worst of it. Whoever it was only gave her a light tap on her neck.'

I twisted my legs to get off the stretcher, and a fire burned through them.

'You need to go to the hospital, Walker,' Sara said as she approached me.

I touched my chest and took several deep breaths. 'Did you catch them?'

She shook her head. 'Did you see who it was?'

Lydia helped me to my feet.

'No. I never had the chance. We were looking through the documents when somebody attacked us. They must have been hiding in the shadows when we got down there.'

Sara had a notebook in her hand. 'Do you know who might have wanted to attack you and Mrs Cross?'

'No.' I tried not to picture somebody turning us upside down for a crucifixion ritual. 'I guess it was just some opportunistic burglars looking for the good stuff in the town's newest building. Kids probably.'

DI Rose scrutinised me with her glare. 'You don't think it was to do with that old photo of Baker you found on the board?'

I rubbed at my head, but the pain wouldn't go away.

'I doubt it. Did you check if it was Baker?' She nodded. 'So it is him in that picture from 1996?'

She removed the photo from her jacket. 'I couldn't find anything to confirm it, but I went back to his house and examined the photos on the walls, and it certainly looks like him.'

'You should get some rest, Frank,' Lydia said.

She was probably right, but I wanted to see Eva first since I'd got her into this mess.

'Do you think it was our killer who attacked you?' Sara said.

'No. As I said, it was likely opportunistic thieves who saw in the media how a rich woman had funded this new building.' At least that's what I hoped had happened.

From the look on Sara's face, I could tell she didn't believe me. She moved closer to me.

'Why are you lying, Frank?'

'I don't want Coe involved in this.'

'Why not?'

'Because he'll come in and take all those documents from downstairs. And he'll waste more time trying to blame me for this.'

'But if it was the Crucifix Killer who attacked you and Cross, it disproves his ridiculous theory about you.'

I tried to shake my head, but it hurt too much.

'I wouldn't put it past him to claim that I staged the whole thing to prove I'm not involved.'

'So you think it was our killer in that basement tonight?'

'It seems the likeliest answer.'

'Then we should add this incident to the official inquiry.'

'No, Sara. I'm unsure if Coe is that incompetent or deliberately trying to foil the investigation, but if that was the murderer, they were there for what's in those boxes. So I don't want Coe taking those documents away before I've looked at them.'

'You mean before we've had the chance to look at them?' Lydia said.

Sara stared at me, and I assumed she was deciding whether to trust me. Then, finally, she put her notebook away.

'What will you do with the files?'

'Well, we can't leave them here. And that's even if Eva lets us take them.'

'You can do what you want with them.'

Eva's eyes sparkled as she joined us, but I could see the attack had shaken her, noticing the dark shadows on her cheeks. My cheek throbbed from where the pipe had struck.

'How are you feeling?' I said.

She touched her neck. 'I'll have a lump for a while, but the medics say I'm fine. How are you?'

I felt the scars on my face. 'I might have lost my good looks forever.'

Laughter snorted out of Lydia.

'Will you take the documents to your house, Frank?' Sara said.

I didn't want to, not with the old man coming home in a few days, but I couldn't see what choice I had.

'My flat's nearby,' Lydia said.

'You don't mind us taking the boxes there?' I said.

She shook her head. 'Nope. I enjoy looking through old photos.'

I smiled at her. 'Okay, thanks for that. We should remove the documents now before anything else happens.'

Sara got out her phone. 'Do you want me to get some officers here to help?'

'No,' I said. 'The fewer people who know where we're taking them, the better. Sara, do you mind staying with Eva while Lydia and I move the boxes to her flat?'

'Of course not.'

I left them in the lobby while I returned to the basement. Strangely enough, the lights were now working. Papers still littered the floor as I looked at the six boxes, which were big enough to contain decent-sized speakers from a home cinema system. Even with Lydia's help, it would take at least three trips to get everything to her place. As I figured out the logistics, she joined me downstairs.

'Are you thinking of carrying all of those on your own?'

'I thought you might help me with them.'

She laughed at me. 'You wish. Anyway, it doesn't matter. I've organised for them to be picked up and delivered to my flat.'

'How come?'

'I called the people who helped me move into the flat, those I trust from the old days.'

'Some of Uncle Tony's goons?'

'Yeah, but they're good blokes. And they have a van.'

As she spoke, two specimens big enough to be heavy-weight boxers came thundering down the stairs. Lydia gave the biggest one a key.

'Take them to my place, Carter.'

He grunted acknowledgement. I moved out of the way

as they picked up the first box. We followed them and returned to Eva and Sara.

'What will you do with the contents?' Sara said to me.

I watched the removal of the files and considered her question.

'I'll become a copper again.'

19   HERE COMES THE SUN

I woke the next morning with my back in pieces and the cat sitting on my chest. At least it wasn't scratching my eyes out. I'd looked after it while Lydia was in Africa for a month, so our relationship was less frosty than it used to be.

It jumped off as the smell of fried eggs and bacon settled on me and soothed my aching frame. As Lydia brought a breakfast plate into the room, I licked my lips in anticipation. However, it wasn't for me. My legs throbbed as I swung them around to get off the sofa, my heart sinking as she placed the food on the floor for the moggy.

'Here you go, Fudge. You need this after listening to our guest snoring all night.'

I yawned and stretched my arms. 'I should have taken the spare bed. Why didn't you wake me after I fell asleep?'

The cat wolfed down the grub. 'I'm not your mother, Frank. And anyway, you looked so peaceful with your thumb in your mouth and curled up like a baby.'

The back of my head pounded as a persistent ache rippled down my spine. And my hand throbbed.

'Can I have a shower?'

'Of course. You know where it is. Get refreshed, and I'll make you breakfast.'

I stood; convinced the cat was winking at me.

'I'll have a strong cup of tea if you've got it.'

I went to the bathroom, stumbling past the boxes we'd retrieved from the community centre. Was the answer to the crucifix murders in one of those? I hoped so, even though I wasn't looking forward to trawling through them.

Lydia had left two large towels for me, but there was no change of clothes. So if I were going to be there for a while, I'd have to go home for supplies.

Home.

Strange how I'd fallen into the trap of calling the old man's house home again.

My father.

I couldn't look through the boxes before clearing my head, and I had to get my dad's situation sorted first. Meaning I had to talk to Kitty Carlisle about organising social services to provide help with his care.

The water consumed me as I thought of him in the hospital, the heat burning into my skin and running over the bruises I'd acquired. The scars on my cheeks vibrated under the temperature as I ran my fingers over them. Might last night's events only have been opportunistic thieves, as I'd said to Sara?

No, it had to be our killer or somebody working with them.

'Don't be too long,' Lydia shouted from the other room. 'Unless you like burnt bacon and toast.'

The water slipped into my mouth, a river flowing into and through me. What would happen with the relationships with my father and Lydia when this was over?

Then there was my brother.

And Eva Cross. Would she return to Australia? Did I want her to stay here? Or was I more interested in Dr Kitty Carlisle?

A thousand and one questions flooded my brain as the water dripped from me, and I turned the shower off. I peered at my weary face in the mirror, seeing lines and cracks that weren't there a week ago. However, that was just part of getting old; the scars on my face and the bruises from last night were different. There was also an extra bit of grey in my hair. I imagined another fifty years of this and wondered if I'd resemble my father.

And would my memory go as well?

There would be nobody to look after me then, as I was caring for him now.

Was that what I was doing? When they discharged him from the hospital, would I be capable of caring for him in his own home? No, and this is why I needed the extra help. But how would he feel about it?

I shook the damp from my head, running fingers through my hair. It was short enough I could push it back, so it stuck up like a toilet brush. Then I flattened it again, so I didn't look too much like an idiot. I dressed and returned to Lydia as she placed a plate of bacon, eggs, and toast on the table.

'Do you have brown sauce?' I said.

'Of course. No sane person has breakfast without it.'

'I used to work with somebody who covered their bacon and eggs with tomato sauce.'

She grimaced. 'What a barbarian.'

I shovelled the food into my mouth and felt better immediately. The cat snuggled up to my foot as I ate, purring against my leg.

'I think Fudge prefers me more than you now, Lydia.'

'That's because you're such a charmer, Walker.' She glanced into the other room where the boxes stood waiting. 'Eva Cross won't forget her first date with you.'

I felt guilty about that. 'I should call her and see how she is.'

'You should. Then what will we do?'

I looked at the clock on the wall. 'Hospital visiting hours start in half an hour. I want to see the old man and check with Dr Carlisle about his discharge. As soon as he's home, my spare time will vanish.'

Even with carers coming in three or four times a day, I'd still need to be there for him.

'So no more hot dates with wealthy widows or running around searching for serial killers?'

'Exactly. Can you do me a favour while I'm at the hospital?'

'Fire away.'

I sipped at the tea, which warmed my mouth.

'Sort the contents of the boxes into photos and documents. Then, with the papers, categorise them in the best way that makes sense to you.'

'Am I looking for something in particular?'

'Yes – any pictures or references to the four victims. See if there is anything that links them together or any connection to the old community centre.' I had one other thought. 'And if there is any mention of the Cross of Saint Peter or Petrine Cross.'

'Is that what Sara mentioned at Baker's house the other night?'

'Yes. It's an inverted Latin cross, used as a Christian and anti-Christian symbol, associated with the martyrdom of Peter the Apostle, who was crucified upside down.'

She bit through a piece of toast, talking as she ate.

'So, you think this might have something to do with the Christian church or maybe some form of Devil worship?'

'I'm not ruling anything out, but the symbolism of the victims being crucified upside down means something to our killer, and we can't ignore that link to the Petrine Cross.'

'Or killers.'

'Indeed. So see if anything in the documents connects to the church.'

'Didn't Sara say the church and the local council used to run the old community centre?'

I nodded. 'The answer must be in those files, which is why somebody attacked Eva and me to get to them.'

'What if they did? What if they found what they wanted and we're just wasting our time now?'

I finished my tea and stood. 'It has to be done. We've nowhere to go with this until another murder.'

'You think that's on the cards?'

'This isn't over, Lydia, even after last night.'

I left her to finish her breakfast and went into the other room to make two phone calls. The first was to Sara, checking if she'd made any progress and ensuring Coe wasn't asking about the events at the community centre.

'We're no further forward, Frank. I'm rechecking the forensic evidence from all four murders while Coe has the rest of the team looking again for connections between the victims.' She paused for two seconds. 'And he's still scouring through your past, searching for a link to the crimes. But, as of now, he doesn't know about the attack on you and Cross.'

'You haven't mentioned the photo of Baker?'

'No.'

I could tell from her tone that she felt guilty about not informing her superior officer. However, it was good news for me. So I told her what Lydia and I would do with the documents and ended the call. Then I rang Eva.

'How are you this morning?' I said.

'Never better, apart from the bruise on the back of my head. You got the worst of it.'

I didn't disagree. 'I'm off to see my father in the hospital before returning to Lydia's. Do you want to meet after that?'

Her silence was not unexpected since I'd guessed the trauma of last night had probably convinced her to avoid me and return to Australia the first chance she got.

But she surprised me.

'Yes, but let's keep out of the public eye. Why don't I come to Lydia's place, and I'll treat us all to a takeaway?'

'That sounds perfect.'

We settled on an eight o'clock start as long as nothing unexpected happened in between. Then I said goodbye to Lydia and ordered a taxi to the hospital.

Kitty was waiting for me when I arrived. 'Are you okay, Frank? You have marks on your face and your hand.'

I touched my cheek, and it felt like the inside of an oven warming up. Was it because of my injuries or my guilt for dating Eva after I'd spent weeks flirting with Kitty?

'I'm fine. I slept on Lydia's couch last night. I think I've cricked my neck, and the cat scratched me.' I hated lying to her, but I didn't want to worry her with the details about the attack in the basement.

'Do you want me to check the wounds?'

I did, but didn't want her asking awkward questions about them.

I smiled at her. 'Maybe later, but thanks for the offer.' I'd turned down the opportunity for her to touch my face, but here I was, flirting with her again. 'Is there any news about my father's situation?'

She reached into her pocket, removed a piece of paper, and handed it to me. As I took it, I got a flash of memory of other papers with my name on them connected to dead men.

'That's the contact number for Jean Warren. She's the social worker assigned to your father. Once you speak to her, you can arrange for the carers to visit him at home. He's ready to leave here when you are.'

'Thanks, Kitty. I don't know how I would have got through this without your help.'

'Have you thought about what will happen when he leaves here?'

'Yeah, but I'm not sure I'm processing it as I should.' Which wasn't a surprise, considering what else I was dealing with.

She took my hand and led me to a seated area. We sat with her fingers in mine. I was convinced it was more than just a professional concern. My heart fluttered, and I wondered if being attracted to two people simultaneously was wrong. I was out of practice. That's what I told myself as she spoke.

'You could take him home and look after him, understanding that his physical and mental health will deteriorate by the day. The second option is for you to stay with him and have carers come into the house three or four times daily, to assist you with his needs. This way, he maintains his usual routine, and you get the professional help he requires. But, with both options, you must know the strain it will put on you both.'

'How so?'

'Well, for people with dementia, each day can switch between lucidity and terrible confusion. And when the confusion comes, it might transform into bouts of fear and pain, manifesting in verbal and physical violence. It's difficult for anybody to witness these, even more so for a relative or a loved one, especially when they don't have the tools to deal with what is happening, and this is where specialist training is required.'

'But there's another option?' I knew there was. I just needed to hear her say it.

'Yes. Your father could go into residential care, where he will have professional help for all his needs twenty-four hours a day. You could still visit him regularly.'

'It's a lot for me to consider.'

'It is,' she said.

'And I'm not sure if we could afford it.' My savings were nearly gone, and even though the old man had two pensions and twenty grand in the bank, I knew it would only go so far with the type of care she'd mentioned.

'Don't worry about the cost for now. Instead, think more about what's best for him and you.'

She was right, and I thanked her. As she smiled at me, I thought again about asking her out. Then common sense got the better of me. I needed to get mine, and the old man's lives sorted first.

I left the hospital as my hunger returned, so I called Lydia.

'Do you want me to bring some food back?'

'I'm starving,' she said. 'But after being cooped up in the flat all morning and with another long stretch to look forward to when you return, I think we should nip out in-between more research to eat.'

'What have you got in mind?'

'I'll meet you at the fish shop opposite the pier in thirty

minutes. We can stare at the sea, and I'll tell you what I've found so far.'

She hung up before I could ask what that was.

Then I told the taxi driver to take me to the beach.

20 LIVING IN A BOX

Lydia was waiting for me outside the chippy, standing at the back of the queue. The breeze was light as the sun stabbed at the scars on my cheeks.

'You don't look any better in the daylight,' she said. 'How did it go with your dad?'

I told her about the conversation with Kitty as the people inched forward.

'She gave me a few things to think about.'

'I still have contacts at Whiteport Council. I can ask about care homes and costs.'

'That would be great, thanks.'

'No problem.' She pointed at my face. 'What did you tell the good doctor about that?'

'I lied. I told her your cat did it.'

Lydia scowled at me. 'That's no way to impress a potential girlfriend, Walker. Lies always come back to hurt you. And it's unfair to Fudge.'

We didn't speak again until we got our fish and chips and sat on a bench opposite the sea. I gazed at the turbines for the thousandth time, imagining them as protectors or invaders. I told her more about my dad as we ate.

Lydia rubbed her hands on her jeans and dropped the paper into the bin.

'It's been a busy morning for me. Do you want to hear what I've done so far?'

I wiped the vinegar from my lips. 'I'm all ears, partner.'

She scrutinised my face. 'So it's official, then? We're partners now?'

'That's if you can drag yourself away from your cat.'

'That's a difficult choice, Walker. Fudge sometimes brings dead rats and birds to me. I don't remember any presents from you.'

We laughed together, finding a rare moment of relaxation amongst the recent turmoil.

'You know I'm more than just good looks, Lydia.'

'All things considering, Walker, you'd have to be.' She reached into her pocket and removed some papers. 'Anyway, I didn't focus on the photos because you're more likely to recognise anybody in them, so I studied what I could of the other documents.' That made sense. 'Even looking through those six boxes, there's more stuff in them than you would have thought possible, so I've only got through about a quarter of it. The biggest problem was of my own making as I spent too much time reading these.'

She showed me the papers.

'What are they?'

'They're letters, from users of the centre to the staff.'

'Complimentary?'

'Most of them are. I'll give you an example.' She scanned the first one. 'This is from a teenage girl praising somebody called Emma for helping her with the kid's school homework. There are a few like this, from different people to various personnel, thanking them for the help, events, and courses the centre provided. I searched for the names of the four victims but couldn't find them. However, I discovered these.'

She handed me two letters. The first was from a mother of three teenagers complaining about their recent treatment at the community centre.

Your staff refused to let my daughter use the toilets, accusing her of selling drugs in the building. My son came home with a cut to his cheek, saying he'd been beaten up in the snooker room, and none of the staff stopped it.

I touched the scar on my face as I read the rest: the mother threatened to write to the local MP if the centre didn't apologise to her and her kids.

The second letter was another complaint, but in a different vein. A resident was unhappy with the noise at night and the gangs hanging around in the street.

These hooligans are selling drugs outside your building and probably inside as well. Unless I receive a satisfactory response from you in seven days, I will inform the police of this behaviour.

I returned the letters to Lydia. 'Is there more like this?'

'A few, but I haven't gone through most of the other documents.'

A woman went past us with a pushchair, screaming at the kid in it as if she'd committed some terrible crime. The noise was loud enough to scare the gulls from the chips I'd dropped at my feet.

'It shows that not everybody was happy with how the centre was run or its staff.'

I pictured that photo with Robert Baker inside the community centre in 1996. Why was a farmer involved with the place back then? Were the other victims connected to it? And what did it all have to do with me?

Lydia stood and approached the sea wall, throwing the last of her fish into the sand. The seagulls swooped and fought over the bits.

'Did you have any luck online with the old photo of Baker I sent you last night?'

She shook her head. 'I couldn't find it anywhere.' It was another dead end. 'Shall we return to the flat and continue with the rest of the documents?'

I agreed, getting up as my bruises sent shivers of electricity through me.

When we got back, the cat was snoozing on the sofa with a leg casually pointing to the floor and the pieces of paper. Lydia scooped them up.

'This is where I was at when you called.'

Most of the boxes were untouched, with a pile of photos on one side and papers on the other.

'I'm going to check the pictures. While I do that, can you separate the letters and sort the other piles into official community centre correspondence – bills, communication from the council or church and things like that – and maybe a miscellaneous pile?'

She nodded, and we got to it.

After an hour, I was still sorting through the photos. It took so long because I was searching for any containing the victims, and it wasn't easy trying to recognise somebody from thirty or more years ago. It would have been easier if there had been information written on them, even just dates and locations, but they were all blank.

I gave up for a break. 'Do you want a cup of tea?'

'Something stronger would be a lot better,' she said.

It was only two o'clock. 'It's a bit early for that. You can make up for it tonight.'

'What's happening then?'

I forgot I hadn't told her about Eva's visit.

'A rich woman is coming to treat us to takeaway food.'

She laughed. 'Your lady friend is the last of the big spenders, Frank. No wonder you fancy her so much.'

The temperature increased on my face and irritated the scars on my cheeks.

'Last night wasn't even a date. And look how horrible it ended. Plus, I guess she'll be returning to Australia soon, so there's no future in it.'

'There's no future in anything, Walker. Didn't Johnny Rotten tell you that?'

'He was a bit before my time.'

She moved the cat out of the way and got off the sofa.

'You're a right cold case when you want to be.'

Before returning to the room, she entered the kitchen to put the kettle on.

'Do you have any biscuits?' I said.

'Oh my God, Frank, that's it. That's the answer to all of this.'

My cheeks throbbed again, and her idea of something stronger to drink suddenly got very tempting.

'What? Our maniac is killing people for biscuits?'

'No, you idiot. I know why Blair's heart was in the fridge with that article about your finest hour.'

I ignored her little dig. 'Enlighten me, oh wise one.'

'At heart, it's a cold case.'

'What?'

'The heart in the fridge is somebody telling us what they're doing is all about a cold case. The murders are a message relating to past events. Something happened to them, and they've never had justice for it. At heart, it's a cold case.'

'That's a stretch, Lydia.'

'You think so?'

The more I thought about it, I wasn't sure. And I needed that drink even more.

'Is this cold case connected to me?'

The kettle boiled before she could answer. She returned to the kitchen to make the tea, and I joined her.

'It has to be linked to you. You were a copper for twenty-five years. There must have been loads of investigations you were involved in that weren't solved, right?'

'Are you critiquing my skills as a police officer, Lydia?'

She poured the boiling water into the cups.

'Don't be daft. You know what I mean.'

Of course I did. 'But those cases happened in London, not here.'

She thought about that. 'Yes, but you're here now.' She put sugar into her drink. 'This is about you being here now, but it's not one of your cold cases.' She beamed at me. 'The Crucifix Killer wants you to solve their cold case.'

I was about to protest, but then I considered her words.

'They planted my name with the last two victims, but not the first two. Why?'

She shrugged. 'Perhaps they did, but it was subtle, and the police never discovered them. That's why they were so extravagant for victims three and four: to ensure somebody noticed them. A plastic bag in the body and a heart in the fridge will do that.'

'But we went with Sara to the first two scenes and found nothing.'

'It might have been too subtle even for you, Frank. We should return to those crime scenes.'

I was beginning to think her crazy theory wasn't so crazy.

'Even if all of this is true, which I won't admit unless we find my name at those first murders, why me? There are plenty of other coppers here, retired or otherwise.'

She grinned at me. 'Christ, you can be so dumb, Walker, for a clever bloke. The reason the killer is communicating with you was in that fridge. Think about it.'

I did. 'The article about Matthews and me?'

Lydia put her drink down and clapped her hands.

'Eureka! But it wasn't any old article, was it? It was all about how you broke police procedures and sacrificed your career to locate the victims of a serial killer. Don't you get it now, Frank?'

I did. 'And you got all this from a heart in a fridge and paper with my name on it?'

'At heart, it's a cold case. Once we find that case, we'll have our killer.'

She was right again. 'I should tell Sara.'

'No. She'll have to inform Coe if you do, and then they'll be straight around here to take those boxes and documents away. We can't have that, not yet.'

The cup warmed my hands as I finished the tea.

'You're on form today, Lydia.' I put the drink down. 'Now, let's hope you can do the same with the rest of those files.'

21 DOCUMENT

I felt guilty for not phoning Sara to tell her what we'd discovered, but the image of Coe's irritating grin convinced me it was best for now. I had high hopes we'd get lucky with the documents, but it was another hour of fruitless searching and half a pack of biscuits before Lydia found something useful.

'Look at this, Frank.' She handed me a printed list of names in one column and cash amounts in the other. 'It's financial contributions to the centre from donors.'

There were thirty names on it, but three stood out:

Robert Baker

Harold Burke

Mark Blair

All of them had donated £500 each.

'We finally have a document that connects the victims, but the journalist, David Cash, isn't on it,' I said.

'Maybe he was involved with the community centre, and we just haven't found the evidence yet.' She dug her hand into the nearest box and pulled out a pile of papers. 'There might be more useful information in here.'

It was possible, and I hoped she'd be right.

'This doesn't mean the three knew each other.'

Lydia nodded. 'True, but it's a start.'

I placed the donation list to the side and agreed.

'We still need to find details of who was involved with the centre from the church.'

'We best keep looking, then.'

So we devoured more biscuits and drank more tea, searching through files that went back to the early 1950s. Frustration ate at me until I found something interesting. It was a yellowing piece of paper from June 1996, the month the old community centre closed for the final time. There was a list of staff, including supervisors and the manager. I put it aside and reached for a note of complaint I'd discovered from one volunteer writing to another, chastising a senior staff member.

Old Bill will get this place shut down when people discover what's been going on here after hours.

I looked at the list, noting the name at the top as the general manager: William Young. I showed both documents to Lydia.

'According to a volunteer, the community centre manager, William Young, was up to no good in the building?' she said.

'Possibly, if we put two and two together and connect Old Bill to William Young.'

She scrutinised the letter. 'Couldn't the term Old Bill be a euphemism for the coppers? So the police would close the centre if they discovered what *he'd* been doing, whoever *he* was.'

It didn't sound right to me. 'No, I think Old Bill has to be the manager, William Young. If we believe this letter, he was doing something he shouldn't in the community centre after it was closed to the public. And that was right before the council shut the building for the last time.'

Lydia peered at that one sentence of text as if she could see some hidden meaning in those few words.

'So what do we do with this information?'

'Would there be anything in the council records, considering they were involved in running the community centre?'

She shook her head. 'While you were at the hospital, I rang one of my contacts at the current council. They said most documents from the 1990s and earlier were destroyed during the changes to local government. Back then, the council covered the whole county, but in the late '90s, the government split it into geographical entities to cover the four major towns: Whiteport, Billsdale, Stanport and Margrove. So that would have been the perfect opportunity to hide something.'

I sat back in frustration. 'Maybe we're overthinking this. The community centre closed in 1996, but I remember that happening to numerous places across the country. The Tory government cut loads of facilities left, right and centre, so it may have been just one of those casualties.'

'You don't think it was because of some covered-up scandal?'

I rubbed at the scar on my cheek. We didn't have many documents remaining to check, and the photos had proved useless. Perhaps last night's attacker took something that would have helped us. Or maybe we were only clutching at straws with this letter.

'Anything's possible, Lydia, but we must find the proof first.' I looked at the papers on the carpet. 'You leave these last few to me and check online for William Young.'

I scrutinised more documents, mostly financial reports, as she scoured the internet. It didn't take her long.

'I got a million hits on his name, most of which are about the singer, Will Young. Then there are teachers, tailors and even cheese makers.'

'What about one connected to Billsdale?'

'There's nothing online about the old community centre, just mentions of the new one. I presume it was too far back for the internet.'

'That doesn't make sense, Lydia. Many people upload information that existed well before the internet.'

She shrugged. 'I guess none of it was interesting enough, and nobody wants to read about cake-baking in the 1970s or look at black and white photos of line-dancing pensioners.'

I returned to the staff list, looking at the assistant manager's name.

'Mary Zimmerman. She must have had regular dealings with Young.' I thought of Bob Dylan, and the David Bowie song about him crept into my head. 'I can't imagine there were many women with that name then or now. See if you can find any mention of her online.'

If not, we'd have to go down the list individually, checking every staff member.

'Unless she got married,' Lydia said as she ran her fingers over her phone.

I puffed out my cheeks. 'And I thought the internet would make things easy when searching for people.'

She beamed at me. 'And you'd be right. I've found a Mary Zimmerman on Facebook. Not only does she live here in Billsdale, but she's also listed herself as a former worker at the old Billsdale Community Centre. And she's online now.'

My heart skipped a beat as I watched Lydia taping onto the screen.

'What are you doing?'

'I'm asking if we could pay her a visit.'

'Telling her what?'

'That we work with Eva Cross, and we're doing a piece on the old community centre to celebrate the opening of the new one, and it would be great to hear her reminisce about it. So I've requested a few minutes for a chat and some photos.'

She finished typing and placed the phone on the floor. We both stared at it in anticipation. Then my mobile rang, and I nearly jumped out of my skin. It was DI Rose, so I answered it.

'How's it going?' she said.

'Nothing yet.' I didn't want to get her hopes up and mention what we were doing.

'Well, I've got some bad news.'

My heart sank. 'Another murder?'

'Thankfully, no, but it's just as unpleasant for you.'

'Coe?'

'Yes. He knows about last night and is sending officers over to confiscate the boxes you took from the community centre. I'd suggest you copy anything of interest and then put everything back. Tell them you haven't had time to go through the boxes when they arrive. They're not going to quiz you. Coe's currently deciding how long to wait before calling you into the station.'

I thanked her for the heads up and ended the call. Then I told Lydia the news.

'We better get to it,' she said.

By the time the uniformed coppers arrived, we'd photographed a dozen items. Yet, it didn't feel like we'd achieved anything as I watched the police take the boxes away.

Then Lydia's phone pinged with a message.

She grabbed her jacket. 'It's on, Frank.'

I followed her out of the flat. 'Where are we going?'

'There's a fishing village nearby, Heaton, and she has a cottage there. It's a five-minute drive.'

I climbed into the passenger seat. 'Did you mention William Young or any scandal?'

'No. I didn't want to scare her off.'

She drove away, and I wondered how to approach this upcoming meeting.

'Do you know how old she is?'

'According to her Facebook page, she's seventy-five.'

'That's around the same age as the victims.'

'You think she might be in danger?'

I raised my hands as she stopped at a red light.

'Who knows? We've got three of them on that donor list, but not the journalist, so there's a connection we're missing. And that's only if we're right about the murders having a link to the old community centre.'

I hoped this old woman could help us catch a serial killer.

Lydia gripped the steering wheel. 'The journalist, David Cash, could have written an article about the community centre or one or more of the other victims. He worked for the local newspaper for thirty years. They could have copies of all of his articles.'

'That's a lot to go through, but we might need to do it if we don't get anything useful from Zimmerman.'

The light changed, and she drove along the coast as I glanced at the boats drifting in the water. Most of the vessels bobbled above the waves, displaying their nets and other fishing equipment, but a bit of each vessel was below, hidden in the ocean. What we couldn't see was just as important or even more than what was visible. I fixed on a boat I'd seen before in those waters, knowing that those who fished there had done so for generations. It sat on the sea with a blazing sun behind it, burning into my eyes. The light was so intense and my mind so full of what I'd looked at all afternoon that its shape transformed to resemble those papers we'd unpacked from the boxes, shimmering there just out of reach and proving useless. We'd got nothing from most of them, but a few, perhaps less than one per cent, had set us on this road.

But would we catch anything at the end of it?

Lydia turned at the end of the road and again a few yards on. It took us down a slight cut to a track that ended before the entrance to the beach. We got out of the car and peered at the little cottages nearby.

'Follow me,' she said.

I did, moving past several dog-walkers and people heading to the sand.

'Let me do the talking,' I said as Lydia knocked on the door.

She frowned at me. 'Yes, boss.'

Thirty seconds later, the entrance opened. A woman with a mop of silver-grey hair smiled at us. She wore a bright purple cardigan, a necklace that any mayor would be jealous of and yellow top and dark trousers. However, I wasn't drawn to any of that, gazing at the crosses in her ears.

No, not crosses – they were crucifixes, with Jesus nailed to both of them.

'You must be Lydia and Frank.' A ginger cat appeared near her legs, and two more followed it. 'I hope you like tea and cakes.'

She led us inside, and Lydia closed the door.

'I love your cats, Mrs Zimmerman,' she said.

'Oh, please, call me Mary. Only the kids ever called me Mrs Zimmerman.'

She took us through a corridor and into the living room. There were no modern electrical devices, computers, TV, radio or anything. Instead, books were everywhere, several of them laid open as if she'd been reading when we arrived, and hundreds on numerous bookshelves. She guided us to sit on a sofa covered with cushions while taking a single-seater opposite. There was a table containing tea, cakes, milk, and sugar, and she poured drinks for everyone.

I peered at the educational books behind her. 'Were you a teacher, Mary?'

'Oh, yes, since I left school to when I retired fifteen years ago. I'm not sure if I'd survive in the cut and thrust of modern education, but I loved my time at the two schools I worked at.'

She didn't add the milk, so I took mine black. Lydia dumped four sugars into hers.

'Did you teach anywhere else?' I said.

Her eyelids flickered as she peered at me. 'What do you mean, Mr Walker?'

Had Lydia told her my surname? I guess she must have.

'Our understanding is that you were the assistant manager at the former Billsdale Community Centre.' Zimmerman nodded. 'Did you do any teaching there as well?'

One cat jumped onto her lap.

'I wish. I loved spending time with the children but never had the chance to do anything but organise the centre's day-to-day running. It was so busy back then with young kids, teenagers, single parents, the pensioners, and several groups who used the building.'

'Were you employed by the council or the church?' I said.

She moved the cat off her lap and leaned down next to the seat, where she retrieved a large binder.

'They threw away many things when it closed, but I kept some mementoes. The centre was open for fifty years, from 1946 to 1996. It was a shame how it ended.' I wanted to ask her about that end, but she handed me the folder. 'You might find some photos of me from my younger days in there.'

I opened it and glanced at the contents. She hadn't answered my question, so Lydia rephrased it.

'Did you work for the county council, Mary?'

She shrugged. 'I didn't pay much attention to who employed me as long as I got paid.'

The dullness in her eyes reminded me of my father, and I wondered how good her memory was. I flicked through the pages, waiting for something to leap out, searching for the names and photos of the victims. And maybe at least one name connected to them.

All the earliest pictures were in black and white, showing the entrance and grounds of the building from seventy years ago, plus its sparse contents. The images reminded me of those my father had; for one second, I thought I might see him and my mother in them amongst those people with far-off faces and sharp clothes. I got through the first few pages, stopping at a photo of a group outside a church.

I showed her the picture. 'Was this the congregation involved in running the community centre?'

She nodded. 'That's the old Baptist church. It's moved now to the other side of town. It was better then since it was close to the centre, so those who attended both had a short walk between them.'

I watched the crucifixes moving in her ears.

'Do you know how the church got involved with the community centre?'

The cat rubbed against her leg. 'From what I heard, the Baptist church leaders approached the council, recommending they work in partnership to create something for the local population to move on from the horrors of the war. So the council funded it while the church added the expertise of some of their members.'

'Were you a member of that church?' I said.

She smiled at me and touched an earring.

'You mean because of these? No, these were a gift from my granddaughter. I think the young people call her a Goth, and these were her idea of a joke. I couldn't have worn these at the community centre.'

'Was that because of the church members?'

Her smile vanished. 'Because of one person in particular; the man who got the place shut down.'

I glanced at Lydia and then looked at Zimmerman.

'Was that William Young?'

The sigh came out of her like a deflated balloon. 'Do you know why it was closed?'

'No,' I said.

'A single council covered the entire region then, but the government divided it into four parts, covering the largest regions. And that meant cuts and job losses. The new Billsdale Council said they couldn't afford the centre's upkeep and asked the Baptist church to take over full control, but they claimed they didn't have the funds. So it was closed, and they converted the building into an amusement arcade. That was the official excuse anyway.' A hint of anger filtered out of her. 'Fifty years of good work and more planned for the future were thrown away because no money was left.'

I sipped at my lukewarm tea. 'But you don't think that was the real reason for the closure?'

She shook her head. 'I knew people at that church, those at the top who ran it. They told me the place was swimming in funds, more than enough to keep that community centre running. So it wasn't for lack of money it closed.'

'So what was it?' I said.

'Silly me,' she said. 'I haven't offered you any cake.'

She reached over and pushed plates towards us. I took a bite from a piece of angel cake.

'It's lovely,' Lydia said. 'Did you bake it yourself?'

'Dearie me, no. My fingers shake too much now for me to make anything.'

'Can you tell us why the centre closed, Mary?'

She sighed, sounding like a tyre running out of air.

'William Young. It was all his fault. I thought he was immature to be the manager – he was in his early thirties and had an impulsive streak. But nobody listened to me until some parents discovered him giving late-night Bible lessons in one of the rooms.'

The light flickered off her crucifix earrings.

'Why would that be a problem?'

'Understand, Mr Walker, that William Young was a fervent fundamentalist Christian who believed everything in the Old Testament was the word of God and cannot be denied.'

'He was an old-time fire and brimstone preacher?'

'To the extreme. He preached that gay people were unholy and needed punishing, that we should run single mothers out of town, and that non-Christians were barbarians. Anybody who didn't believe as he did was blasphemous, and the penalty for that was severe. Immigrants, atheists, anyone who supported abortion – his list of undesirables was lengthy, and he spoke against them in that building for months. In addition, in his congregation were many young people who repeated his words outside of the centre. However, not only kids attended his sermons – several influential individuals were part of Young's fundamentalist community: police officers, politicians, lawyers, teachers, and business leaders. It would have developed into quite a scandal if it had got out. There was a rumour that a reporter for the local paper was writing a story on it, but that never appeared.'

My heart thumped against my ribs. 'Was the journalist David Cash?'

She shrugged. 'I don't know; it was just what I heard.'

'Do you recognise the names Robert Baker, Harold Burke, or Mark Blair?'

She gazed straight into my eyes. 'Of course I do.'

I nearly knocked my teacup over. 'Did you see them at the community centre?'

She laughed at me. 'No, Mr Walker. I saw their names in the newspaper. Some horrible person murdered all of them.' She touched her earring. 'Crucified upside down, I read.'

Was she messing with me, this woman in her seventies?

'You'd never heard of their names before seeing them in the media?'

'Is that what this visit is about? You think something connects their deaths to the old community centre?'

'Were any of them part of William Young's Bible group?' Lydia said.

'Not that I'm aware of, love, but I never saw his congregation, only learning about it later from other people.'

'Who took the final decision to close the place?' I said.

'Somebody from the council, I guess.'

'What happened to William Young?' Lydia said.

'His church banished him, his family disowned him. He even lost his job. I think he had to move from the area, but I don't know where he went after that.'

I chewed on the cake and pondered her words. Was she keeping information from us, and was it deliberate or the possible result of dementia?

I stood and smiled at her. 'Thank you for your time, Mary. It's been very helpful. And the cake was great.'

We said our farewells, and we left the woman with her cats. When we got outside, I didn't go straight to the car, instead heading in the other direction towards the small fishing boats in the sand. I strode onto the beach and saw the dog walkers and tourists enjoying the sun. Lydia joined me.

'What did you make of all that?'

'How old would William Young be now?'

'Mary said he was in his early thirties in 1996, so I guess he'd be in his late fifties.'

'So, still healthy enough to crucify somebody upside down?'

'Sure, especially if he had help.'

'But why? And why now?'

We trod across the beach as she spoke.

'You heard what she said. He lost everything – his

church, community, family, friends, home and job. That would be sufficient to trip anybody over the edge, especially if they were already teetering on it.'

'Okay, maybe. I've known people kill for less, but why wait until now?'

'There could be many reasons. He might have been out of the country or even in prison.'

I leant against a boat. 'And you've had no luck tracking him on the internet?'

'Not yet. We could go into the online census records to see if we can track where he was living.'

The sea breeze drifted over me as I peered at the horizon, but all I saw were Mary Zimmerman's crucifix earrings winking at me.

Were the victims crucified upside down like Saint Peter because of William Young's fundamentalist Christianity? Were they part of his congregation? And were those particular men killed because Young somehow blamed them for his troubles? If that was true, were there any more people on that list?

And what did any of it have to do with me?

I looked at my watch – it was nearly six o'clock. 'Eva's due at yours in two hours.'

'Do you need all that time to get ready for her?'

I laughed. 'I'm wondering if we should tell Sara what we just heard.'

'All I know is I want a drink right now.'

'Before Eva arrives?'

'It's called an apéritif, Frank.'

'It's a goofy teeth.'

'What?'

'That's what my wife used to call it.'

Her eyes bulged as she stared at me. 'So what happened to you two?'

'It's a long story.'

She trudged out of the sand towards the road.

'Okay, I need a drink now so you can tell me all about it.'

I went with her, glancing at Mary Zimmerman's window, those crucifixes still burning onto my retinas.

23   TONGUE TIED

We had two beers each while we waited for Eva. The knock on the door came half an hour earlier than expected at seven-thirty. It was a surprise to see Sara there when I opened the door.

'Have you come for the free food and booze?'

She pushed past me without an invitation. Lydia was sitting on the sofa, stroking the cat.

'Are you chasing after Walker as well, DI Rose?'

Sara frowned as I slumped next to Lydia.

'Yes, but not for what you think.' She glanced at the bottle of beer in Lydia's hand. 'Are there any more of those going?'

Lydia pointed at the kitchen. 'In the fridge. Help yourself.'

Sara went and got one as my stomach rumbled.

'Am I in trouble again?' I said as she returned.

'The MIT went through those boxes with little luck,' Sara said.

Lydia looked perplexed. 'MIT?'

'The Murder investigation Team,' I said. 'The Senior Investigating Officer runs it.'

Lydia frowned. 'Coe?'

Sara nodded. 'And he's not happy with you, Frank. He thinks you probably removed items from those boxes and didn't return them to us. Is that true?'

'Of course not. We copied anything of interest, which wasn't much, and then put everything back where we found it. Isn't that true, Lydia?'

She agreed. 'Scout's honour, Inspector Rose.'

'I doubt you were ever in the scouts, Lydia.' Sara removed her phone from her pocket and showed me what was on the screen. 'Is this a document you copied?'

It was the donation list containing the names of three of the Crucifix Killer's victims.

'Yeah, but the journalist isn't on there.'

She put her mobile away. 'Did you find anything else useful?'

I finished my drink and took Lydia's empty bottle from her.

'Do you want to recount our trip to the Zimmerman house while I get refills?'

'Sure, partner.'

I heard Lydia relate the details of our afternoon excursion while I was in the kitchen. Fat fingers clawed at my guts as I returned, amused by the strange look on Sara's face.

'So you think William Young is our killer?'

'Or one of them,' I said. 'I still believe this is at least a two-person operation.'

Sara sipped at her beer. 'I agree with you on that, but I need to see more evidence to convince me that Young is involved. There are too many unanswered questions regarding him: if losing everything he held dear turned him into this upside-down crucifix killer, why has he waited so long?'

Lydia repeated what she'd mentioned earlier. 'Perhaps he's been out of the country or even in jail.'

'She's right,' I said. 'The main thing is we need to find him.'

Before either of them could reply, Lydia's phone pinged. She checked the message.

'Eva is running late, but she says the meal should be here soon and hopes we like Indian food.'

Sara grabbed at her stomach. 'I haven't had a good curry in a long time.'

Right on cue, somebody knocked on the door.

'Don't you have a bell, Lydia?' I said.

She stood. 'I do, but nobody ever uses it. Walker, I might have to put a picture of your face over it to get people to press it.'

Sara laughed. 'Careful, Lydia, you don't want to scare folk away.'

Lydia got the food while I went to the kitchen for the plates and cutlery. Five minutes later, we were sitting around the table enjoying the takeaway delights as the cat looked at us through jealous eyes.

'You're not getting any, Fudge,' Lydia said. 'You know it makes you shit everywhere.'

Sara pointed her fork at me. 'What's going on between you and the wealthy widow?'

I chewed on a piece of curried broccoli. 'Whatever do you mean, Detective Inspector Rose?'

'I believe she might be jealous, Frank,' Lydia said.

Sara spat rice onto the floor. The cat devoured it before Lydia could intervene.

'He wishes.' She looked at Lydia. 'Unless you think I'm interested in Eva Cross?'

Lydia smiled at her. 'Are you?'

'The money would be nice.'

Lydia agreed. 'Indeed. Frank, isn't the wealthy widow a bit old for you?'

I could see the two of them were having a grand time winding me up.

'She's my age,' I said.

'Did she tell you that?' Lydia said. 'Because I couldn't find much information about her online.'

'Yeah, I think so. Anyway, what does her age matter?'

'Indeed,' Sara said. 'It's not how old she is that matters, but how much she has in the bank, right, Frank?'

'Ha bloody ha.'

I finished the beer and went for another one. While in the kitchen, I lingered there, wondering about Eva Cross. After all, I hardly knew the woman, and she'd be heading back to Australia sooner rather than later.

Lydia and Sara were laughing; no doubt at my expense, when I opened the fridge. That's when I saw a beating heart next to the bottle. Underneath it was a piece of paper, and I realised what was on it. The scar on my cheek throbbed as I rubbed it. The smell of the curry had disappeared, replaced by an aroma of flesh and blood.

I took a deep breath and blinked. The heart was gone, and I grabbed three beers. The other two giggled like schoolchildren when I returned to the living room.

'I'm glad somebody's enjoying themselves,' I said.

Sara took my spot on the sofa and scratched the cat's chin.

'I can't remember the last time I relaxed like this.'

'You should get a cat,' Lydia said. 'They're much friendlier than humans.'

They slumped into each other as if they'd been best friends all their lives, the copper and the niece of a local gangster. And there was me watching them, the former detective inspector wondering where my life was going. Perhaps I just needed to stop thinking about the future and focus on the present.

Yes, once I got the old man sorted.

Sara pulled the cat onto her lap. 'I think you're right, Lydia. This is all I need to keep me warm at night.'

She glanced at me as she spoke, and I would have sworn she was sending me some message. But I'd never been that good at uncovering coded communications, as this latest investigation had proved.

I took the seat opposite them. 'Has Lydia told you her theory of why my name was left at the last two crime scenes, Sara?'

'Describing it as leaving your name is putting it mildly,' she said. 'Your name was on a piece of paper in a plastic bag the killer forced the victim to eat. And the other one was on a printed article in the fridge underneath the victim's ripped-out heart. But, no, she hasn't explained this theory to me.'

'The Crucifix Killer wants Frank to solve a cold case for them,' Lydia said.

Sara scrutinised me. 'This is because of what you did in London with Christopher Matthews?'

'That's what Lydia thinks.'

Sara nodded. 'Okay, but if so, why didn't we find your name at the first two crime scenes?'

'You can't have looked hard enough,' Lydia said. 'We need to recheck them both.'

'That's not a problem.' Sara looked at me. 'But if we're

stitching all these theories together, you believe William Young has murdered four people as revenge for what happened to him in 1996? And, correct me if I'm mistaken, he's left Walker's name at two murder scenes to prompt Frank to right the imagined wrong done to Young twenty-six years ago. Is that correct?'

I reached for a piece of nan bread. 'When you say it aloud, it doesn't make much sense.'

'Don't get me wrong,' Sara said. 'I think you might be right about Young as our killer, but the other bit with your name as his prompt for you to clear his name doesn't add up.'

She was correct. 'Are you going to tell Coe about William Young and our theory?'

'I already have,' Sara said. 'I texted him the details when you were in the kitchen.'

I could only anticipate this causing me more problems. 'What did he say?'

'He hasn't replied, but since I told him it came from you, I'm assuming it hasn't gone down well.'

The bread nearly stuck in my throat as I laughed. I was struggling to jolt it out when the doorbell rang.

Lydia jumped up. 'See, it does work.' She opened the door and dragged Eva inside. 'You're just in time before Frank eats everything.'

Eva smiled while Lydia took her coat.

'I'd have been here sooner, but I got a visit from the police.' All three of us stared at her. 'An unpleasant man called Coe interrogated me in my hotel about the attack at the centre. He also wanted to know what I knew about the contents of those boxes.'

Lydia handed her a glass of water. 'Drink this while I warm the food for you.'

Eva took Lydia's vacant seat. 'Thank you. I'm hungrier than I thought I would be.'

'Are you okay?' I said to her.

She nodded. 'I am, but this Coe specimen doesn't like you, Frank. He said some terrible things about you.'

'Like what?'

'He thinks you're involved in what the media calls the Crucifix Killings and that I'm in danger being around you.'

If Coe had been in the room with us, I'd have strangled him there and then.

'Inspector Coe is under a lot of stress,' Sara said. 'I'd take his theories about Frank with a pinch of salt, Eva.'

'With a pinch of salt?' I said. 'So you think some of his theory is true, Sara?'

She shrugged. 'Well, you are connected to the murders. And if you and Lydia's theory is true, it's a significant connection.'

'What theory is that?' Eva said.

Lydia brought Eva's food and answered that question while I nipped off to the toilet. I stayed there longer than needed, letting Eva digest more than the grub. What would she think if a serial killer was communicating with me because they wanted my help?

And why did I care what she thought?

'It's an interesting theory,' Eva said as I returned. 'But have you given any more attention to the method of the murders?'

'The upside-down crucifixions?' I said.

Eva nodded. 'Yes. It seems like a lot of trouble to kill somebody, even for revenge. There has to be a deeper meaning to it than that.'

I told her what we'd discovered about The Cross of Saint Peter.

'So the murderer believes his victims to be unworthy?' Eva said.

'I think it's more than that. I'm assuming the killer perceives his victims as unworthy compared to him. That would make sense if the killer were William Young, who, from what we've heard, likely believed himself to be the direct voice of God. Then Baker, Burke, Cash, Blair and whoever else took all that away from him. Or so he believes.'

Sara looked at me. 'Whoever else? You're assuming there will be more victims?'

'Yes, I'm guessing it's not over. There were a lot of names on that donor list.'

'But not the journalist,' Lydia said.

That omission was still stumping me. 'No. We must go to the local paper to look through their archives.'

'Thirty years' worth?' Eva said.

'I don't think so. Young lost everything in 1996, so we might need only to check that year.'

Eva ate as she spoke. 'Is there nothing about him online?'

'There's plenty,' Sara said. 'But none of it's useful. It's the same with the former solicitor and assistant chief constable.' She looked at me. 'I've asked Coe if we can access Blair's police work record and visit the firm where Burke worked. I'm waiting for him to get back to me on those.' Then her phone rang. 'Speak of the Devil.'

She got up and went into the kitchen. The cat followed her.

Eva turned to me. 'How's your father?'

'Better. He should come home soon.'

'And you'll be looking after him?'

'I guess so.'

She reached over and touched my arm.

'Losing a loved one is the worst thing in the world. You never get over it.'

I felt I should ask about her recently deceased husband, but was unsure how to brace the subject without putting my foot in it.

Then Sara returned.

'That was Coe.' I knew from the look on her face it wasn't good news. 'There's been another crucifix murder.'

'Where?' I said.

She gripped her phone. 'Close to here, in the Baptist church.'

The cat ran out of the room as an imaginary smell of fire and brimstone overwhelmed my senses.

We left Lydia and Eva in the flat as Sara took me to the crime scene. As she drove, I looked at my phone, peering at the copy I'd made of the donor names.

'Who's the victim?' I said.

'The minister, Leonard Gibson, seventy-eight years old.'

'He's not on the list.'

'I know, but didn't you tell me it's this church that ran the original community centre with the council?'

'Yes, it is.'

She pulled up near the building. As we got out of the car, the curry taste lingered in my mouth, and I saw Coe talking to a uniformed officer. Several SOCOs were standing outside, and I wondered if anything was wrong inside: something worse than an upside-down crucifixion.

I approached the church and the circle of gravestones that formed the entrance. My legs froze as I got there, the hesitation generated by the sudden realisation I might see my father's name on a headstone soon. I went to the closest one, running my fingers across the top, letting the surface cut into my skin. We'd been estranged for most of our lives –

a situation created by his poor parenting and my rebellious nature – but I couldn't bear the thought of seeing his name engraved in stone in a place like this.

A gravestone, something so cold and immovable, should never mark a person's existence. What lies in the ground was once only flesh and blood, but all of us were much more than that. We are the memories of all those lives we've touched, for good and bad, and we are the infinite emotions we create every day of our lives. I wasn't religious, but deep inside me was the lingering belief there had to be more to life than what we did in this world.

The name on the gravestone had faded with time; 1888 marked the date of death. Maybe a tree with a wind-chime in the branches would be more appropriate for the dead, or a digital screen replacing the stone, where one click would display the highlights of their life to a recording of their favourite music. I liked that idea and wondered what an electronic memorial to me would be: nothing from my child-hood and teenage years – perhaps a brief mention of how I disfigured my brother – instead focusing on my time in the Metropolitan Police. The soundtrack for that would be Primal Scream and The Happy Mondays, while PJ Harvey could describe my brief marriage to Alisha.

Alisha. I hadn't thought of her in such a long time. We were one of those couples who were better before we married, happiest when no responsibilities were weighing us down. I wondered what she was doing now, knowing I was only thinking about her because another woman was monopolising my thoughts for the first time since she'd left.

Two women, in fact: Eva and Kitty.

Was there any future with either of them? Eva would likely return to Australia, and I wasn't sure how Kitty felt about me. Maybe I was better off on my own, anyway.

The sound of somebody throwing up in the cemetery dragged me from my reverie. I heard the retching as the wretched Coe stormed towards me, with his cheeks all puffed out and his face redder than a tomato.

'Where have you been all day, Walker?'

'Hello to you as well, Coe.' I wasn't about to put up with his crap anymore, especially not in public.

Sara stepped between us. 'Frank's been with me for the last hour. Before that, he was with Lydia Thompson.'

She looked at me for confirmation, and I nodded.

Coe ignored her. 'I have a witness placing you in this location this afternoon.'

'Lydia and I visited a house around here to see Mary Zimmerman. Would you like the address?'

'Yes. Give it to an officer.' He turned to Sara. 'Do you still want him looking at the scene?'

She nodded. 'I do.'

'Okay. Get the protective gear on, and I'll take you in. I'm keeping forensics back until we've finished inside.'

'Who found the body?' I said.

He pointed at the bloke bent over a gravestone, spewing his guts. 'That poor git.'

I studied the church, examining the centuries-old brickwork that matched the graves in the cemetery. The churchyard was immaculate, not a speck of rubbish apart from the guy's fresh vomit. A uniformed copper led him away as I climbed into a yellow plastic suit resembling a reject from a 1950s science fiction movie.

The protective clothes were uncomfortable on me – I was out of practice wearing them – but I wriggled inside as I followed Coe and Sara into the church. The smell assaulted me first, a mixture of raw sewage and dirty cat litter alien to the religious sculptures and paintings that greeted us.

Hundreds of flickering candles lit the way as I took a deep breath and stepped into the corridor between two sets of pews.

Inside, the arches loomed in the shadows, towering over me like a dark, vengeful deity. Between them, the stained-glass windows displayed the birth and death of Christ. I peered at Jesus on the cross as the hairs rose on my neck. The chill in the air cut into my skin as I saw what was waiting at the end. Sara gasped and clutched at her throat. Coe stood there as the colour drained from his cheeks. He strode before us, and we followed, with Sarah glancing at me as we went.

Coe wiped the sweat from his forehead. 'As you can see, this differs from the other crime scenes.'

That was putting it mildly. Gibson was naked, crucified upside down like the others, but unlike them, nailed to a cross. And there was more.

A river of blood covered the ground, with hundreds of flies buzzing over the body. Somebody had removed the skin from his cheeks and head, showing nothing but blood and bone. All his internal organs lay on the pews on either side of him, displayed neatly in rows. The eyes bulged out of a skinless face, the mouth wide open.

And they'd castrated him.

Sara coughed and leant on the nearest pew. I stood there as the curry taste in my throat transformed into something else. Now I understood why the bloke had thrown up amongst the tombstones.

'Where are his genitals?' I said.

Coe turned to me. 'We haven't found them yet.'

Sara steadied herself. 'Are there other similarities to the previous murders?'

'You mean have we discovered any reference to Walker?' Coe said. He stared at me as if he was Medusa trying to turn me into stone. 'Not yet.'

I wasn't sure if that was good news or not. 'Why are you keeping the SOCOs back?'

'I didn't want anything moved before you cast your beady eyes over this horror, Walker.'

I couldn't tell if he thought I'd have some helpful insight or because he assumed I'd incriminate myself. As it was, I did neither. Instead, I gazed at the surrounding horror, wanting none of it and reluctant to get into the mind of anyone who'd do such a thing.

Still, I moved closer to the body, ensuring I avoided the river of blood on the ground. I peered at the fleshless skull, wondering how long it had taken him to die.

'This is an escalation,' I said.

Coe snorted. 'You think?'

I glared at him. 'What do you want me to do?'

His laughter echoed through the rafters. 'Dazzle me with your insight, Walker. You're a skilled investigator, so tell me what you see here.'

All I saw was blood and horror, picturing my name on a gravestone nearby. So I turned and left, trying to push the images out of my head and failing miserably. Then, outside, I removed the protective clothing and dumped it in a bin.

Sara followed and did the same next to me. 'What do you think, Frank?'

'What do I think? I think you want to find my name somewhere in there.'

Coe joined us. 'And why is that?'

My bones ached as I peered at him. 'Whoever did this doesn't need to talk to me anymore. They got my attention, and I'm here. Now, this is all about completing whatever their ultimate goal is.'

'Why don't they need to talk to you anymore?'

'Because, Coe, they believe I've listened and understood them. I'm only here to ensure that, when this is over, the police and the other authorities won't paint all of this as just another lunatic on a meaningless killing spree. There's a method in this madness, and they want me to explain it to the rest of the world.'

He gazed at me as if I was a carnival exhibition.

Then he burst out laughing.

'Christ, and you accused me of spouting nonsense. You're so full of yourself, Walker, you can't even smell the shit coming out of your mouth.' He pointed at the road. 'Now, get off my crime scene so I can let the forensic team inside.'

I didn't argue and headed towards the car. Sara stayed with Coe, so I walked back to Lydia's place. If the killer wasn't communicating with me anymore, was there any point in involving myself in the investigation? I pondered that question during my stroll along the coast while peering into the sea and observing those guardians standing deep in the ocean. The lights flickered on them as if they were sending out a message, another one I didn't understand. By the time I got to the flat, Eva was gone. Lydia was slumped in front of the TV, watching a programme about UFOs.

'How did it go?' she said.

I grabbed a beer from the kitchen and told her everything.

She grimaced. 'The violence has skyrocketed. What does your experience tell you about that?'

The bottle chilled my fingers. 'It means if we don't catch them soon, it will only worsen.' I sipped at the booze. 'Was Eva okay?'

'I think so. She left ten minutes after you and Sara. She said she'd call you tomorrow.'

Half the beer slipped down my throat, and it suddenly felt like I hadn't slept in an age. 'Can I stop here tonight?'

'You can stay as long as you want, Frank.' The cat must have agreed since he crawled into my lap. 'What will you do next?'

It was a question I didn't have a proper answer to, but I tried my best.

'Let's see how I feel when I wake up. Sara and Coe don't need us in their investigation now, and I've got more pressing concerns.'

'Your dad.'

I nodded. 'I have to speak to social services to arrange for his care. Then he can leave the hospital and come home.'

'Do you want to talk about this latest murder?'

'Maybe tomorrow. I'm ready for bed now.'

I finished the bottle and grabbed another as Lydia retired to her room. The cat followed her and gave me a curious look as it went. I looked forward to getting some sleep, as long as the image of that body eviscerated on the cross didn't haunt my night.

25 FUTURE PROOF

I crawled out of bed, close to lunchtime, but at least I hadn't spent the night on the sofa. Every part of me ached, but my mind felt refreshed. Lydia had gone out and left a note.

I've taken Fudge for a walk. Help yourself to anything you want.

I wasn't hungry, so I showered and dressed. Then I checked the news on the TV and online, searching for the latest information on last night's murder but finding nothing new. The sun was blazing through the window, convincing me to get some fresh air. Lydia had left a spare key on the table, so I took it and locked the door behind me.

I had two choices: walk into town or return to the crime scene. The smell of blood lingered in my head, so I headed down the coast. It was thirty minutes to get to the Baptist church. The police cars and officers were still outside, and I wondered if they'd been there all night. There was no sign of Coe and DI Rose. I sat on a wall on the opposite side and called Sara.

'Afternoon, Walker.'

'Are you in the church, Sara?'

'No, I went this morning, but I've done everything I can there now.'

'Did you find anything connected with me?'

'No, Frank, your name was absent from the crime scene. However, we discovered hundreds of Bibles in a small room, so Coe has got officers going through every page searching for any mention of you.'

'Looking for the Devil?'

'I guess so.'

There was silence between us for thirty seconds.

'Is there any progress in the investigation?'

She sighed down the line. 'We're in the exact spot as we were last night.'

'No luck tracking down William Young?'

'Nope. He seems to have disappeared when he left Billsdale in 1996. We haven't found any mention of him online. Do you still want me to take you and Lydia to the first two crime scenes again?'

'There's no point, Sara; we know why the Crucifix Killer left my name at the other crime scenes.'

'So you'll solve some old cold case?'

'I guess so, though I'm not going to do it. I'm finished with this now. You and Coe can deal with it all. I've got my father's situation to sort out.'

'Okay, I understand. I'll keep you informed, and you let me know what happens with your dad.'

'Will do.'

I sat for five minutes after the call, watching the officers wandering in and out of the church. They moved through the cemetery, and I wondered how many more graves would be dug before this was finished.

Nevertheless, as I'd told Sara, this didn't involve me anymore.

I got up and returned to town via the beach. The sand was soft underfoot, and the sun caressed my face. When I reached the end of the pier, I saw Lydia holding a long lead with the cat at the end. Plenty of dog walkers used this stretch of coast, but they kept a wide birth from the moggy.

'Aren't you worried about the dogs?' I said.

She grinned at me. 'They recognise when to keep away from a predator, even when it's a cat.'

I glanced at the people on the beach, watching the mutts chase each other while avoiding Fudge.

'You've been around predators, Lydia. Do you think you know how to spot them before they act?'

'You're talking about my time with Uncle Tony's business empire?'

The laughter hurt my chest as it burst out of me.

'Business empire? Is that what you called it?'

She pulled the cat closer to her to keep it from a crab crawling out of the sea.

'Who's the predator there, Frank? Fudge or the crustacean?'

'That's different, Lydia. They're not human and only act on instinct. They don't torture or kill living things for fun, as humans do.'

The moggy was straining at the leash to get to the crab.

'You're wrong, Frank. Fudge isn't hungry and doesn't want to eat the crab. Instead, he wants to play with it, just like he does with mice, birds, or squirrels. He won't with dogs because they're bigger than him.'

I went to the cat and peered into its curious eyes.

'So, you think Fudge knows where he is in the hierarchy

of living things and seeks smaller creatures to torture and kill because he enjoys that?'

'Contrary to what some might say, no human can ever know what's in the mind of a cat or any other creature. Hell, we don't even understand why our own minds function the way they do most of the time.' She bent her knees to stroke the moggy. 'But I've been around Fudge long enough to know why he does what he does. He wants to control the crab because it's smaller than him, unaware of how its claws and shell work. I'm not keeping him from it for the crab's sake, but for his. We do the same with people we care about; protecting them from those we believe might harm them. So, to answer your question, there were several predators employed by my uncle, and I knew when to steer others away from them.'

'But not from you?'

She smiled at me. 'Do you think I'm afraid of predators?'

'No, Lydia, I don't.' I watched as a wave swept the crab back into the water. 'But is it possible this Crucifix Killer is only doing this because they're a predator who enjoys torturing and killing people, and there's no special meaning to their methods or for leaving my name at the crime scenes?'

'I thought you'd finished thinking about this?'

I shrugged. 'I keep trying, but something is nagging at the back of my head that won't let it go.'

She picked the cat up. 'Predators, Frank. This is all about predators. And you're very good at catching them.'

We headed from the beach, and now I was hungry.

'Is it time to eat?' I said.

'Sure. Let's return to the flat, and I'll make you lunch.'

AN HOUR LATER, I relaxed on the sofa after Lydia had cooked us pasta and vegetables. Fudge was on my lap, licking his lips.

'Have you made a decision regarding your dad?' she said.

'I rang the hospital this morning. The nurse said he was stable, and I said I'd go over during visiting hours after six. Because of his dementia, the doctors had to inform social services, who designated a social worker for him. I've arranged to meet her in Whiteport in an hour at four o'clock.'

'Do you want a lift?'

'That would be great, but what will you do while I'm there?'

'Don't worry about me. I'll wander around the town. Then we can visit your dad together in the hospital.'

So we had the rest of the day sorted.

'I'll take you for a drink afterwards, Lydia. I want to try that wine bar at the end of the pier.'

She agreed, and we spent the afternoon drinking tea and eating snacks. I kept away from the TV, internet and my phone, consigning the Crucifix Killer to the shadows of my mind.

Lydia dropped me off outside the social services offices near Whiteport Town Hall. It was a new building, and not the one I remembered from my teenage years. That was still there on the other side of town, standing empty, as it had done for three decades. I went inside to reception and asked to see Jean Warren. The receptionist told me to wait, so I sat in the corner for five minutes.

Then a tall woman who looked close to retirement age greeted me.

'Mr Walker?'

'Call me Frank,' I said.

She shook my hand and led me into a room. In it were two chairs and a table with a laptop on it.

'Would you like a drink, Frank? Tea or coffee?'

'Water is fine.'

We sat, and she poured two glasses. Then she opened the computer, and the screen came to life.

'I've spoken to the doctors and your father. Are you aware of the current situation?'

'I believe so. The hospital will discharge him soon, and I need to organise care for him. Is that right?'

She nodded. 'That's correct. Have you decided what type of care you want for him?'

'I understand we can have four visits a day?'

'Yes: morning, lunch, teatime, and early evening.' She wrote on her notepad. 'Is that what you would like?'

'Yes. I'm out of work now, but I hope to get a job soon.' I wasn't sure if that was true, but I was running out of money, and I wouldn't claim any benefits. 'So I'd like to get something in place ASAP.'

'Do you have a date for your father's return?'

'Today or tomorrow.' Kitty said he was ready to leave, so there was no point in waiting any longer.

She wrote again. 'Good. Once you have a definite date, call me, and we'll arrange a time for me to visit him.'

'Visit him?'

'Yes. I have to see him at home and talk to your father, so I can decide what help he needs. So, will he require assistance in the bath or shower? Does he need somebody to do his shopping, cooking and cleaning? If so, we must ask him what he likes to eat. Once we have all the relative information, we'll create the correct care package for his needs.' She put the notebook on the table. 'Have you discussed this with him?'

'Yes,' I lied. 'What about the cost?'

She grabbed a small card from the desk and handed it to me.

'Do you have access to the internet, Frank?' I nodded. 'Great. Go to the website on that card and fill in your father's details, including his financial information, and it will calculate the costs. Depending on his circumstances, he might not have to pay anything.' She looked straight at me. 'Do you contribute to his cost of living?'

The scar on my cheek vibrated with heat. 'No, I don't.'

Her smile was one of embarrassment for me.

'Okay, Frank. Do you have any other questions?'

'No. I think that's everything. I'm going to the hospital now.'

We stood together, and she offered me her hand, which I shook.

'Well, call me as soon as you have a discharge date for your father.'

'I will.' I slipped the card into my jacket and left the building, feeling not much better than when I'd entered.

Outside, I gazed across the town, pushing back the memories clawing at the sides of my head. I got the phone from my pocket, ready to call Lydia, ignoring the temptation to check the news. I had no time to think about dead men when I had to focus on getting my father home.

And the police hadn't found my name at the newest crime scene. The killers were obviously escalating, and once that happened, they would likely get sloppy and make a mistake. Then it would only be a matter of time before Sara cracked the case, even with that idiot Coe in charge. She was more than capable of dealing with the investigation and compensating for Coe's incompetence.

If Lydia was right and the killers had left my name at two murders to spark my involvement, they were in for a tremendous disappointment.

My father's health was more important than why five men were tortured and murdered.

Lydia came with me to the hospital. I thought she might want to wait outside, but she seemed keen to see my father. I assumed she might have felt guilty about how her uncle treated the old man, but I told her she wasn't responsible for Tony's behaviour. She nodded without reply, but it must have played on her mind how he'd hidden his drug dealing and child slavery from her.

A nurse ushered us onto the ward, the familiar smell of antiseptic and hospital food assaulting my nose. My father was at the end of a row of four patients, men of the same age, who all looked like they were waiting for the next world to welcome them. He sat up in bed and smiled as we approached. I wondered if he remembered who I was or if the dementia had worsened.

'Hello, Frank. Have you come to take me home?'

I took his hand, the wrinkles on his skin reminding me of tree bark and glanced at the nurse.

'Maybe tomorrow, Dad.'

His smile vanished as he peered at Lydia. 'Mary, will you take me home?'

Mary was the daughter he hadn't seen in nearly fifty years.

'That's not Mary,' I said. 'That's my friend.'

The old man's eyes glazed over as he gazed at Lydia. 'How do I know you?'

She took the seat next to the bed and rolled up her sleeve. 'Do you remember this, Mr Walker?'

My dad and I stared at the tattoo, a colourful dragon covering the inside of Lydia's arm from the elbow to her wrist.

He grinned at her. 'Of course. You're Lydia, the tattooed lady.'

It surprised me to see her ink, but then my father did something I'd never seen or heard him do before. He sang.

> *Oh Lydia, oh, Lydia, say have you met Lydia*
> *Oh, Lydia, the tattooed lady*
> *She has eyes that folks adore so*
> *And a torso even more so*
> *Lydia, oh, Lydia, that encyclopaedia*
> *Oh, Lydia, the queen of them all*
> *On her back is the Battle of Waterloo*
> *Beside it the Wreck of the Hesperus too*
> *And proudly above the waves*
> *The Red, White and Blue*
> *You can learn a lot from Lydia*

AS HE SANG, he waved his hands in the air, and I stood there with my mouth open, catching flies. It was as if I'd been transported to a mirror world where everything was reversed. His eyes sparkled, and there was a shine to his smile I'd never seen before. Where had this man been all of my life?

Lydia grinned. 'What's the matter, Frank? Cat got your tongue?'

The old man lowered his voice but continued to sing and stare at the wall.

'Well, I didn't know you had a tattoo.' I glanced at my father's beaming face, delighted to see him happy. 'So how come my father did, and what's this song he's singing?'

She shook her head. 'You're such a philistine, Walker. This is *Lydia, The Tattooed Lady,* famously sung by Groucho Marx in the movie *At The Circus.*' She narrowed her eyes at me. 'You have heard of Groucho Marx?'

'Of course I have. He invented Marxism.'

Lydia laughed so hard she had to put one hand on her chest.

'Okay, I'm not sure if you're messing with me, but your dad, as I assume you know, is a big fan of the Marx Brothers, and he taught me the song when he knew I had this tattoo.'

I vaguely remembered watching old black and white comedy movies as a kid.

'And when did he make this fascinating discovery?'

'It was two weeks ago when you were shopping, and I took him to the park. He was telling me about your wasted childhood, so I told him about getting this on my recent travels.' She pointed at the ink on her arm. 'He remembered the song, and I found it on YouTube. The rest, as they say, is history.'

My father had stopped singing, but the revelation still flabbergasted me.

'So, you're the girl with the dragon tattoo?'

'You only know that from the movie, don't you, Frank? I'm assuming you've never read a book in your life.'

The old man spoke before I could reply. 'Who's taking care of me when I get out of here?'

Lydia laughed. 'Don't worry, Mr Walker, I'll make sure your son looks after you.'

Confusion swept over his face. 'Thomas? Is Thomas here?'

My heart sank as I stared at this frail man. In an instant, anguish had replaced his happiness. Would carers be able to provide him with a decent quality of life now his mind was shrinking daily?

But that was the only choice I had. I couldn't look after him on my own even if I stayed at home every day, which I couldn't since I needed a job. Placing him into a full-time residential care setting was a no-go as I'd seen how most of those places work. The thought of him ending his days in such a place made me nauseous. We'd had no proper relationship for most of my life, but I'd never do that to him. So now, I had to explain the new situation to my father while he was still thinking about tattooed ladies.

'Dad, when you return home, some people will visit you every day to help out. How does that sound?'

'People, what people? Is Colleen coming to see me?'

Colleen was my other sister who hadn't visited her father for four decades. I felt resentment against her and Mary even though I'd done the same as them, avoiding the old man, for most of my adult life.

Was it fair to tell him his daughters wanted nothing to do with him and his oldest son was in prison? Wouldn't it be better to let him believe his children were still there to look after him rather than knowing it was a bunch of strangers being paid to do that? At that moment, I couldn't imagine what harm it would do to let him think that.

'We'll see when we get you home, Dad, but you won't be on your own anymore.'

His eyes glistened as he spoke. 'What if I want to be on my own?'

Lydia laughed and touched his arm. 'I'll kick them all out of the house for you, Mr Walker.'

He reached over and put his other hand on hers. 'What's your name, love?'

'I'm Lydia, Mr Walker, Frank's friend. Remember Lydia, the tattooed lady?'

His fingers trembled, and I thought he'd start singing again. I wanted him to sing again and see that happiness on his face once more.

He ran a hand over hers. 'Any friend of Frank's is a friend of mine, Lydia, so you can call me Jack.'

'Okay, Jack, I want to show you something.'

She removed her phone and found the YouTube app. I sat in the corner and watched Lydia show him the wonders of the internet. We stayed with him for forty minutes before he tired. He was sleeping as we left, and I spoke to a nurse.

'Is tomorrow okay for your father's discharge, Mr Walker?' she said. I nodded. 'If everything is fine after the doctor has completed her rounds in the morning, we'll arrange for him to go home. Somebody will contact you to confirm this.'

I thanked her, and we strolled out of the building.

'What now?' Lydia said.

It was just before seven, and I needed a drink. Sara hadn't been in touch, and I couldn't be bothered calling her. All I wanted was to relax for the evening.

'Do you fancy a beer in that pub at the end of the pier?'

She nodded. 'Sure, I like that place. I'll drop you there first because I need to head to the flat to sort Fudge out. So you can get the drinks in.'

It sounded good to me. She drove back while whistling the *Tattooed Lady* song.

Lydia dropped me outside the bar as the sun slipped below the horizon on the sea.

'I'll see you soon,' I said as she headed to her flat.

Flickering lights illuminated the seafront, turning the night into a Las Vegas pastiche. The aroma of fish and chips filled the air as the sound of Elvis singing *Hound Dog* burst out of a nearby arcade. My mouth was as dry as the beach, and I was looking forward to that first drink. I was picturing the bottle in my hand when I heard the cries of somebody in trouble. It came from the seawall gap leading down to the water. I ran to it, stopping to see four young men towering over a bloke on the ground. Two of them kicked him in the stomach as I went over. I reached for the nearest thug and pulled him to me. He looked at me through startled eyes before I tossed him into the sand.

'What's happening here, lads?'

They turned and scowled at me together.

'Fuck off, old man. This has nothing to do with you.'

'Four against one doesn't seem fair, so why don't you leave him alone and bugger off to the arcade?'

The biggest one flexed his knuckles and glared at me. 'Now you'll get a beating just like that fuckwit.'

I stepped in and punched him in the nose. It cracked with a satisfying sound as my hand throbbed. He staggered backwards and fell over the bloke on the ground. The other two froze in surprise.

'Get lost, lads, and I won't hurt you.'

One of them was foolish enough to lunge forward, only stopping when I kicked him in the knee, and he dropped like a stone. I glanced at the three of them cursing in the sand. The last one standing wasn't as stupid as the others, helping his fallen comrades up. They hobbled together and scowled at me.

'You can't stop all of us at once,' the leader said.

I shrugged. 'You've got off lightly so far, lads.' I flexed my sore hand at them. 'Do you want to risk spending the night in the hospital?'

Arrogance fuelled my words, but I didn't feel that confident. They whispered between them as I wondered if I would pay for my bravado. Then they swore at me in unison and turned away. I heard them swearing as I picked up the man they'd attacked. Blood was on his face and a mark on his cheek, but I recognised him: Jim Furman.

'Thank you,' he said.

'You look like you need a drink,' I said.

He wiped the blood from his lips.

'I owe you one.' He nodded at the bar. 'Will that place do?'

I agreed as I watched the thugs cross the road. Would they return with more goons? I wasn't sure, but I knew I couldn't leave Furman on his own. And I needed a drink.

The pain diminished in my knuckles as I wondered what else the night would bring me.

We entered the bar together, finding the place half-full and darker than the far side of the moon. An aroma of pepperoni pizza lingered in the air while the Rolling Stones drifted out of the speakers. Furman bought two bottles of Mexican beer, and we grabbed a table away from everybody else. I squeezed into a seat, the fading leather rubbing against my throbbing legs.

He raised his bottle to me. 'To your health, and thanks again.'

'No problem,' I said. I took a large gulp, enjoying the cold liquid hitting my throat and tasting the lime in the alcohol. 'I thought you would have headed home after the opening at the community centre.'

His eyelids flickered as he drank. 'Home?'

'Wherever you live. I assumed it isn't here or in Whiteport anymore. Or do you have family there?'

'No, my parents came with me when I moved to Manchester in 1991. They're in their seventies now, but they still live there.' He scrutinised my face. 'Aren't you from Whiteport?'

I downed half of the beer in one go, enjoying the tang as it nipped the sides of my mouth.

'I was born there in 1977 and left twenty years after that. So my first visit back was a few months ago.'

'Ah, so you're two years younger than me. I wonder if we ever crossed paths in our teenage days and never knew it.'

'I suppose it's possible, but your life must have been nothing but keeping fit and playing football while I was too busy getting up to no good.'

'You were a bit of a tearaway, then?'

'No more so than any other teenager.' I gazed at the fresh mark on his face. 'I got all the fighting out of me then.'

He grinned at me. 'You're talking about those thugs knocking me down, aren't you?'

I shrugged. 'It's none of my business.'

A group of young women dressed as dominatrixes marched into the bar clutching inflatable penises as the music changed to Abba's *Dancing Queen*. They stumbled around the room, and I wondered if the venue did table service.

Furman glanced at the new arrivals as he cradled his drink.

'Those lads were winding me up, so I told them to fuck off. It didn't impress them.'

'Some people are jealous of other's success.'

Surprise sprang from his eyes. 'Success? Oh, you mean my brief professional football career?'

'Few get to play for Manchester United at the highest level, no matter how short it was.'

'Maybe, but that wasn't what those lads said to me. It wasn't what they taunted me about.

'You don't have to explain it to me.'

He slumped in the seat before pulling himself back up.

'I've kept this inside me for so long, Frank. Perhaps it's time to talk.'

I finished my beer. 'If you think it will help you, then sure. But let me get another round in first.'

I left him to think about it and went to the bar. One dominatrix tapped me on the head with a plastic penis and gave me a drunken smile. I grinned but didn't speak. While I waited for the beer, I sent Lydia a message.

Hang back for a bit, as I need to give somebody a shoulder to cry on.

She replied with an okay, and I took the drinks to the table. Furman had a quick swig of beer and glanced at the group of women who'd started singing an obscene version of *Living Next Door To Alice*.

'I think you might have made a new friend there, Frank.'

The woman from the bar was waving the inflatable appendage at me while dancing with her mates.

I turned from her. 'I'm far too old for anything more energetic than a quiet drink.'

Furman shook his head and laughed. 'Are you a football fan?'

I shrugged. 'Not really. I'll watch England if they're in a proper competition, but that's about it.'

'But you know how my career ended?'

'Some thug kicked you in a pre-season friendly game. As a result, you broke your leg and never recovered to play again.'

'That's the gist, and nothing was ever said about it outside of the club. One second I was a rising star, pipped to play for England; the next, I was all but forgotten. I tried to get fit again, but it was impossible. The club helped me into university in Manchester, and I went into teaching after that.'

The pain in his voice drowned out the women singing along to Boney M's *Rasputin*. My apparent admirer was Cossack dancing in the middle of the room while pink plastic penises floated to the ceiling.

'I imagine working with teenagers is harder than playing professional football.'

'To some extent, yes, but it's much more rewarding. Well, apart from the difference in pay.'

I laughed with him. 'Money isn't everything.' Yet I was running out of it. 'So those thugs weren't goading you about your injury?'

He took a deep breath. 'Oh, they were, but not because my career was over before it began.' The music increased in volume, but he kept his voice low. 'They were repeating a rumour football fans have spread about me for thirty years.'

His expression told me this was something he'd held inside him for a long time.

'You don't have to tell me.'

Furman glanced at the group of women as they stopped dancing and bought more drinks. One stood on a chair and tried to grab the floating penises hovering above them.

'I do, Frank. I need to get this off my chest for my sanity.'

The bottle chilled my fingers. 'Okay, I'm listening.'

He moved closer to me so I could smell the blood lingering on his cheek.

'Everybody thought it was the other player's fault I broke my leg in that challenge, but it wasn't: it was mine. He said something to me, the same things those lads shouted at me outside, and the red mist came down. So I charged at him in that tackle.' He paused for another taste of beer, wiping a finger across his top lip before continuing. 'I tried to break his leg, but it backfired on me.'

He stopped talking and finished his bottle. I peered into his eyes, knowing he wanted me to ask the question.

So I did. 'What did the player say to you?'

'He said I enjoyed being fucked by my dad.'

A chill ran through me. 'What?'

'You're a similar age to me, Frank, so what do you recall happening in this town, in this county, in 1990?'

'1990? I was thirteen, listening to The Happy Mondays, Primal Scream, and Betty Boo. Or I was sneaking into the cinema to watch *Total Recall* and *Brain Dead*. I don't remember much else about that year.'

But I did. Far back in my mind, I knew what he was talking about, something we'd all chosen to forget, an event that had cast a dark cloud over the area for many years.

The child abuse scandal.

His eyes narrowed as he scrutinised me.

'Really? Still, I guess you're in the majority for forgetting what happened here that year.'

'What's this got to do with what those thugs said to you tonight and what the footballer said three decades ago?'

His hands trembled as he gripped the empty bottle.

'Think back to 1990, Frank, and what happened here. In the space of a few months, the authorities took hundreds of youngsters from their parents in terrifying raids. Some were placed in foster homes, but they removed so many kids from families that social services ran out of places for them. So they forced the most unfortunate children to stay in a local hospital ward. And I was one of them.'

The chill from my spine spread through the rest of me like a virus, awakening memories long since forgotten.

'I remember it now, of the kids talking about it at school.

My mother told me to avoid some family who lived at the bottom of our road because the council had taken their two daughters away. I think they were allowed home eventually.'

Furman nodded. 'Most of the kids were, including me. A paediatrician and his assistant at Whiteport Hospital referred over five hundred children to social services in the first few months of 1990. That number increased during the rest of the year. The sudden escalation of alleged child sex abuse cases led to a panic that received nationwide coverage. The four towns involved, Whiteport, Billsdale, Stanport, and Margrove, became household names for child abuse. I don't know how the opposing player in that football game knew I was one of those kids, but he did. That's when I went crazy.'

I sipped at the beer, needing something more substantial to ease my mind.

'But weren't all the allegations false?'

'Most of them, yes. The two paediatricians who started the whole business used an unproven medical diagnosis that was later discredited. Yet, social services and the police took the children away.' He stopped talking as the dominatrixes stumbled out of the bar. 'I'm part of an online group of those taken from their families, and I can tell you the trauma cuts deep into us. Child protection agencies, social services, the police and the courts were all found at fault, but a large portion of responsibility landed at the door of the lead paediatrician. But he wasn't punished and left the county to keep doing the same job at the other end of the country. His assistant quit medicine but stayed in the area.' He pushed the bottle from him. 'When Eva asked for my help, I said no at first. I'd tried to put the whole thing behind me, knowing that coming back would resurrect all those terrible memories. It has, but I'm glad to talk about it at last. And I'm glad she asked for my help.' I watched as he relaxed, and a smile crept across his face. 'And before you ask, no, my parents never abused me. I'd climbed onto the shed roof in the garden and then, like an idiot, fell off. That's why I was in the hospital covered in bruises, and Dr Carlisle and his assistant misdiagnosed me.'

Something invisible attached itself to the back of my throat. 'Dr Carlisle?'

'Yeah.' Furman's eyes darkened. 'God, all the kids hated him and the other one for what they did to us. Somebody said on the internet forum he died a few years back.'

I struggled to breathe. 'Did he have a daughter?'

'I don't know. I heard his wife left him when the whole thing blew up, and the scandal went nationwide.'

A sudden overwhelming dread consumed me, and I got up.

'I've got to leave. Will you be okay?'

'Sure. Have I upset you?'

I shook my head. 'No, I just remembered something I have to do. If you're staying in town, give me your number, and we'll go for a proper drink soon.'

He told it to me, and I put the details into my phone, struggling because my fingers trembled. Furman looked at me as if I'd drank too much, but that wasn't the reason.

'I owe you a meal for saving me,' he said.

'That sounds good. There's a decent Indian restaurant around here.' I was about to leave when an idea sprang to the front of my brain. 'Do you recall the name of the other paediatrician, the one working with Dr Carlisle?'

His grimace unnerved me. 'None of us will ever forget that. It was Dr Baker.'

I had to stop myself from sprinting out of the bar.

The night air hit me like a sledgehammer, irritating the scars on my face and pushing me towards the gap in the seawall leading to the beach. The phone was in my hand, calling Sara as I leaned against the wall. She answered it immediately.

'It's a good job I'm working late, Frank, or I'd assume you were stalking me.'

'Robert Baker, what did he do before buying that farm?'

'Er, a good evening to you as well, mate.'

'I'm not messing around, Sara; this is important. Do you know what Baker did before he became a farmer?'

'Well, technically, I don't think he was a farmer. He bought the land and got other people to work it for him. Where are you going with this, Frank?'

'When did your parents move to Whiteport, Sara?'

I could hear her thinking on the other end of the phone.

'1985. I was born here two years later.'

'So you were three in 1990?'

'That's some excellent maths skills you have there, Walker.'

'Did your parent's ever talk to you about the child abuse scandal of 1990?'

There was silence for thirty seconds. Then, 'What's this about, Frank?'

'Do you have Mark Blair's police details near you?'

'Some of them. A lot are still in sealed files. I've gone through them with a fine toothcomb three times and found no connection to the other victims beyond what we discovered on the community centre's donor list.'

'What position did he hold in 1990?'

'Let me check the screen. Here we go: he was a detective sergeant based in Whiteport.'

The wind whistled off the sea, blowing up sand that clung to my cheeks like a second skin. I used my free hand to brush most of it away.

'Is there any mention in his records if he was an officer involved in removing hundreds of kids from their families?'

The sudden realisation of what I was implying must have hit her then.

'Christ, Frank, you don't think...?'

'Just check, Sara.'

The silence enveloped me like a tomb. As I waited, I watched people enter the bar and heard the sounds of those enjoying themselves. I wondered if Furman was still in there, trying to drink away the trauma that had engulfed him for over thirty years.

And I thought about my mistakes.

Had I got it wrong about the Crucifix Killer all this time?

'According to the information I have on the screen, DS Blair wasn't involved in what happened to those children, Frank.'

The waves covered the steps leading from the beach up

to the bottom of the wall, moving in and out like the turbulence inside my guts.

'Could they have kept the details from his permanent record?'

'Yeah, possibly, but even if he were involved, he would only have been one of many. There were dozens of coppers dragged into that mess, so why kill him and not the others?'

I ran my fingers along the wall behind me, the concrete rubbing against my skin and drawing blood.

'I don't know, Sara.' I watched the blood drop from my hand. 'Is it possible to check where Harold Burke worked to see if his firm was involved in any legal requirements regarding removing the children from their families?'

'Probably, Frank, but it will have to wait until tomorrow.'

Frustration ate me up. 'Okay. We need to do that and study the local paper to see if David Cash covered the story.'

'What about Leonard Gibson?'

'The same with him. We'll speak to people at the church; see if something connected him or that church to the scandal in any way.'

'What's prompted this line of inquiry, Frank?'

I told her about my meeting with the footballer. 'The timing fits. It's just a few years earlier than we were looking at.'

'So you don't think it's to do with William Young anymore?'

'I'm not sure. We can't rule anything out, but I believe we should pursue this connection to the 1990 child abuse scandal for now.'

'And you want me to tell Coe this?'

'I suppose you'll have to.'

'I suppose I will. What are you doing at the moment?'

'I'm going to Lydia's to explain everything and settle my aching brain. She might find something useful online now we have a different avenue to investigate.'

'Okay, Frank. Enjoy the rest of your night.'

She ended the call, and I put the phone in my pocket. Enjoyment was as far away from me as those wind turbines standing in the sea. I started walking towards Lydia's flat when I saw the lights on in the community centre.

Could whoever attacked Eva and me have returned there?

I ran across the road and peered through the window. It was brighter than the sun inside, but there was nobody there. I tried the door, finding it locked.

So I continued to Lydia's.

That was until somebody tapped me on the shoulder.

I spun around, expecting trouble, and my hands turned into fists, assuming those four thugs had returned.

Eva grinned at me. 'Are you stalking me, Frank?'

I relaxed my fingers and laughed. 'I have thought about it.'

She laughed with me. 'Stalkers should never be encouraged, Mr Walker. As a former police officer, you should know that.' She removed a set of keys from her jacket. 'They've finished the commemorative wall in the community centre and added a dedication to me. Would you like to see it?'

'Of course, but I thought you'd be avoiding the building after what happened the other night.'

'You can't run from the past, Frank; you must face it head-on.' She wrapped her arm around mine. 'Plus, I've got you to protect me.'

Eva opened the door, and we went inside. She locked it behind her as I peered at the wall of photos and posters.

'They've done a good job,' I said. I stared at the spot where I'd seen the old photo of Baker. It was empty now as she led me to the display.

'They are a dedicated bunch of volunteers. I'll miss them when I leave.'

I turned to face her as she hung onto me. 'You're not staying then?'

'My work is nearly done, Frank. I've got nothing to keep me here now.'

I didn't know what to say. I thought of her, and then I thought of Kitty.

Dr Carlisle. Was she related to the Dr Carlisle involved in the scandal in 1990? And was Robert Baker the second paediatrician like Furman had claimed?

She guided me to the board of photos, and I saw her name in large text at the top.

'The staff wanted to celebrate my generosity, so they insisted my name go up in big letters.'

'Quite right as well,' I said.

I scrutinised the images, realising there were new ones there – pictures I hadn't seen when trawling through those boxes of documents. One colour photo caught my eye. It was inside the old community centre, a picture of kids sitting in front of a stack of books.

She gripped my arm. 'I've never lost my love of reading, even now after the trauma of the last few years.'

I inched nearer to it, my guts churning with each move-ment of my legs. In the middle of the teenagers was the unmistakable smile of Eva Cross. When I stared at the names underneath the kids, it said Eva Green.

Of course, Eva Cross was her married name.

She pulled me closer to her, my lungs drowning in the aroma of her perfume, which smelled like fresh flowers.

'You never said you used the old community centre.'

'I didn't come here much, just for the book club once a month. It was my brother who loved the place.'

'Your brother?'

'Paul. He was three years younger than me, but we were as close as two siblings could get.'

That sinking feeling threatened to submerge me. 'Was?'

'Yes, Paul died in 1990.'

I wriggled from her grasp. 'What... what happened, Eva?'

'Haven't you put it all together yet, Frank? You were here in 1990.'

'The child sex abuse scandal?'

She wiped at her eye. 'I'd already left home and was working as a chambermaid in a hotel in Berwick. So imagine my surprise when my parents phoned to tell me the council had taken Paul from them because they believed he'd been abused. It was nonsense, of course. He'd fallen down the stairs, and my mother took him to the hospital. Dr Baker was the one who examined him – the monkey, not the organ grinder – and that's when everything went to hell.'

My mind and heart struggled to stay in focus.

'Did you come home?'

'No, I couldn't. The hotel wouldn't let me leave, and I would have lost that job if I'd gone without permission. And it was hard finding work in 1990. My mother said it was all a mistake and that the council would send Paul home soon.'

'Did they?'

'No. I didn't know most of this then, only learning of it years later when my mother was on her deathbed in Australia. My husband had passed away a month before.

Cancer took both of them. Before that came her revelations, including things she'd never told my father because she was too embarrassed.'

'Social services found your brother a foster home?'

'Yes, and not just any old one – it was the home of an upstanding community member. Nobody was worried about him living there. Nobody but my parents. My father went to our local police officer, begging him to do something about it. The copper said he would as long as my father paid him. So he did, handing over all of their life savings, over five thousand pounds. That's about fifteen grand in today's terms. My mother tried everything, speaking to a solicitor representing families against the council. But he only worked for middle-class families, not working-class ones like mine. She told me she got down on her hands and knees in his office and begged him. He laughed at her in front of his staff. I can't imagine what that was like for her. And then there was the journalist.'

'David Cash?'

Eva shuddered. 'I can never say his name. Just the mention of it makes me want to vomit.'

'What did he do?'

'My mother didn't tell my father about this, ever. A rumour was going around that he was planning an article about the truth of the situation. My parents were desperate then, so she tried to speak to him at the local newspaper offices, but she could never get through the front door. The solicitor had reported her behaviour to the police, and they leaked to the press that some parents – the ones allegedly abusing their kids – were threatening people to get their children back. I don't know if other parents did that, but mine didn't. So she visited the journalist at his home. He said he'd help her if she did him a favour. Can you guess what it was?'

Phantom fingers clawed at my insides, pulling away blood, bone, sinew, and organs.

'Cash forced her to have sex with him?'

Eva's eyes were nothing but dark pits now. 'He made her do the most degrading things for months while promising he'd get an article in the paper to tell her version of the events. But of course, he never did. Instead, once he'd finished with her, he tossed my mother aside like a dirty rag.'

Her words sank into me like lead, wanting to crush my bones. I knew of only one thing to say to her.

'I'm sorry, Eva.'

'There's more, Frank. It must have been terrible for all of those parents – not only were their children snatched from them, but they were accused of the most heinous crimes. But do you know why my parents tried so hard to get their son back?'

'In his foster home – somebody was abusing him?'

'Can you believe the irony of it? The council and the police, under the instruction of two paediatricians, removed my brother from his family because the doctors claimed my parents were abusing him. Of course, they weren't, but the authorities placed him with a foster family where the husband inflicted such pain and abuse on Paul that the shame forced him to take his own life a month after returning home. In the scandal's aftermath and its reporting in the national media, nobody was too bothered to wonder why a sixteen-year-old boy would kill himself. Of those who questioned it, the answer always came back: Paul did it because he'd returned to those who'd molested him and wasn't that why the daughter had left as well?'

I gazed into her eyes, understanding how foolish I'd been. I didn't know what to say to her. She was a killer or the partner of one, and that realisation froze my vocal cords.

Then I remembered what I'd seen in that church.

'Baker was the second paediatrician; Burke the solicitor who ridiculed and reported your mother; Blair was the copper who took your family money, and Cash was the journalist who abused your mother.' She nodded. 'So you murdered them for revenge, but what about Gibson?'

Darkness filled her face. 'Can't you guess who it was that social services, in their infinite wisdom, thought would be a good foster home for my brother?'

The final domino fell into place. 'Leonard Gibson.'

'Indeed. For who would think a church minister could harm a child?'

I closed my eyes, seeing Gibson upside down, castrated with his guts on the ground between the bibles.

Then I opened them to see insanity peering back at me.

'Why have you waited so long, Sara?'

'I told you, Frank; I only discovered all the details when my mother revealed them to me last year. I wanted to go to the authorities, but I had no proof, and who would pursue a case against the perpetrators now, after all this time? Then two things happened that set me on this current course. First, I discovered a group online dedicated to people who'd suffered from the scandal, of the families and kids still hurting from those unjust accusations, some of which continue to follow them. I spent a long time there, listening to the hate members had for those who'd created their suffering. So many people were shouting for violent retribution, but I realised none of them could do it. Then someone posted a link to Dr Carlisle's death, and I knew what I had to do. Carlisle had died in his sleep. After moving to the other end of the country, he'd had a successful career and was well-loved by everybody in his community. It didn't seem fair to me that somebody who'd caused so much pain and anguish could live a life like that. One other user voiced the feelings I'd kept to myself, so I sent them a private message. It didn't take long for us to hatch our plan.'

'Why crucify them upside down?'

Her eyes shimmered as she spoke. 'They had to suffer as much as possible for what they did.' She smirked at me. 'And I'd read a book about a crucifix killer on the plane journey here from Australia.'

I wasn't sure if she was messing with me or not.

'You said two things set you on this murder spree.'

'All in good time, Frank. Have you got any other questions for me?'

I stared at the photos on the board. 'What happened in the basement here?'

'I had to remove a photograph from those boxes. Unfortunately, I failed to talk you out of visiting the centre that night.'

'But they attacked you as well.'

'A necessary bit of pain. My partner couldn't hit you and not me without raising suspicion.'

'And you did that for what?'

She removed a photo from her pocket, a faded image of two teenagers, a boy and a girl.

'This is the only picture I have of us together, so I couldn't lose it. I'd hoped to have access to those boxes before the centre opened, but it wasn't to be.'

I looked closely at it, recognising the younger version of Eva and guessing who the lad was.

'That's Paul?'

Sadness consumed her face. 'It is. Don't you know him? I felt sure you would.'

She moved closer to me. Should I grab the picture and restrain her? And where was the partner?

I scrutinised the photo, seeing a teenage boy with a shock of curly blonde locks.

'I don't recognise him, Eva.'

'Think of him with shorter dark hair. He had it cut and changed the colour after I took this photo.'

Then it came to me.

'Paul Green! He was a big punk fan.'

'So you remember him?'

I stared at the picture, imagining him with different hair in the playground.

'Vaguely. He kept to himself at school, from what I recall.'

'He wasn't one of your friends?'

'No, Eva. So, is this why you left my name at two crime scenes?'

She shook her head. 'Your name was at the first four murders, Frank. I knew the police were too dumb to see it at the first two, but didn't you examine them?'

'I did. There was no link to me there.'

'On the farm, didn't you look through Baker's record collection?'

'No. Why would I do that?'

'Oh, Frank; I bet you would have if you were still a copper. Baker's records were all jazz albums apart from one: Scott Walker's *Climate of Hunter* album with his first name crossed out and replaced with yours.'

I pictured the inside of Baker's place, remembering Lydia looking through his record collection. Eva was correct; I'd been lazy.

'What about the second crime scene at Harold Burke's house?'

'It was a book: Alice Walker's *To Hell With Dying* with

your forename replacing hers. That should have stood out since Burke was a noted bigot. But, unfortunately, I had to cut out the subtlety when that didn't work and go for the direct route.'

'Making sure my name was in the stomach?' She nodded. 'But why? I told you I didn't know your brother even though we went to the same school.'

'That's not what my mother told me. She said Paul came to you for help, but you ignored him.'

'That's untrue, Eva. I don't know why your mother said that, but she was wrong.'

'You would say that, but there was another reason I wanted you involved in this.'

'You want me to tell the world what happened to your brother and your family.'

'And what happened to all the others, Frank. None of them has had justice. So a respected ex-copper like you will be listened to when you explain why I did all this.'

I shook my head. 'It doesn't matter now, Eva. I'm calling the police.'

'Even though you don't know who my partner is.'

'We'll find them eventually.'

'What, before they kill Dr Carlisle?'

'What?'

'You heard me, Frank. Unfortunately, the man who caused so much pain for hundreds of people got away with it, so his daughter should pay for his crimes.'

'Where is she, Eva?'

She nodded towards the basement. 'Downstairs. Would you like to see her?'

I pushed past her, running through the door, not stopping until I reached the basement, seeing Kitty Carlisle bound and gagged on a chair in the middle of the room. I moved towards her until a figure stepped out of the shadows and placed a knife at her throat.

Jim Furman brushed at the mark on his cheek. 'Eva said there was no need to crucify her, but I enjoyed doing the others. And she has to pay for her father's crimes.'

Eva came downstairs. 'I couldn't have done it without his help. The logistics of turning a body upside down and keeping it in place is difficult. We tried using tape initially, but that was hit and miss. Yet we got there in the end.' She moved next to me. 'And now we come to the finale.'

I had to keep her talking and figure a way of getting that knife from Kitty's throat.

'Earlier on, you said two things set you on this path. What was the second one?'

Her smile gave me goose bumps. 'Are you trying to delay the inevitable, Frank?'

'No, Eva. I don't like loose ends.'

'Well, it's an end, but it's not loose. The cancer that killed my mother is hereditary, and I have less than a year to live. It's amazing what humans can do when we have nothing left to lose.'

'So now you're going to kill Kitty, is that it? I can't condone what you did with the others, but I understand it. But what happened to your brother, to your family, has nothing to do with her.'

I glanced at Furman, gambling if I could get that knife without him harming her.

Eva laughed at me. 'Kitty? Is there something between you and her, Frank?' She moved from me towards her captive. 'And there was I, thinking you were interested in me.' She ran her fingers through Kitty's hair. 'Or did you want something to happen between you and her?'

'You won't get away with this, Eva. I've told Sara everything.'

'I don't think so. You only put it all together when you came here and saw the photo of me on the board. And what do I care, anyway? I'm dying.'

I looked beyond her to Furman. 'What about you, Jim? Are you willing to go to prison?'

He grinned at me. 'Nobody knows of my involvement. Eva's prepared to take the fall and keep me out of it. It's the way it has to be. The authorities would have covered it all up, if we'd gone to them. Now, Eva gets her day in court where she can tell all of our stories: all those who were hurt by people who should have done better.'

I returned his smile and reached into my pocket. Then I removed my phone and held it up.

'That might have worked if I hadn't set this to record the second I stepped into the building.'

'You're lying, Frank,' Eva said.

'You won't know unless you take this from me.'

She turned from me and looked at Furman. 'Give me the knife and get the phone off him.'

He hesitated, lifting his gaze from me to look at her.

It was all that Kitty needed.

She leapt up, taking the chair with her and thrusting her head into Furman's arms. He fell back and dropped the blade.

That was my invitation to move.

I punched Furman in the face. Then I aimed for the neck, catching him in the throat. He gasped and blacked out. Before turning around, I gave him a cursory glance to ensure he was unconscious. Eva was gone. I cut Kitty's bonds from her and made sure she was okay.

She nodded. 'What about her?'

'She won't go far.' I called Sara. Coe was going to love this. 'How did she get you here?'

Kitty wiped at the marks on her wrists.

'I don't know how she got my phone number, but she called me and said there was something I needed to know about my father, information about the scandal he was involved in.'

'You knew about that?'

'Of course. My father never forgave himself for it. It was one reason I became a doctor and returned to my hometown.'

'You were born in Whiteport?'

She nodded. 'I was three years old when we left.'

'Didn't anybody remember the surname when you went to work in the same hospital?'

She shook her head. 'Nobody was remaining from my father's time. So if anyone recalled the name, I guess they never associated me with him.'

The phoned connected at the other end.

'Sara, have I got a story for you. You need to bring Coe to the new Billsdale Community Centre.'

We were walking up the stairs as I told her the details. I stopped talking when I saw Eva lying on the floor. Lydia was standing over her, with the cat on a lead at her feet.

'You took your time,' she said.

Relief seeped out of me. 'What are you doing here?'

She pulled the moggy closer to her. 'I was walking Fudge when I noticed Cross bring you in here. I watched the two of you talking and knew something was up. Then she led you into the basement, and I realised I'd better get in here. So I picked the lock.'

I saw the glint in her eyes. 'You thought we were heading down there to have sex, didn't you?'

Lydia grinned. 'I was going to throw Fudge onto you and see what happened.'

As Eva groaned on the floor, I burst out laughing.

Then we waited for the police to arrive.

I WAS SITTING on the seawall peering into the waves when Sara left the community centre and sat next to me.

'Furman is singing like a bird.'

'I guess he's kept so much bottled up inside for so long he can't help himself now,' I said. 'Is he saying anything interesting?'

She nodded. 'He's confirmed what you told me. He met Eva online in the forum for those affected by the child abuse scandal. I think she groomed him for this, but he didn't take much convincing.'

The song of the sea rocking against the wall didn't ease the ache in my brain.

'So, Baker was a consultant paediatrician for social services along with Kitty's father, Dr Carlisle. Those two started the whole thing, with hundreds of children dragged from their families based on a test to establish child abuse that was later discredited. Baker quit medicine and went into farming while Carlisle moved from the area.'

'Carlisle went to Cornwall after his wife left him, getting a job with the NHS there,' Sara said.

'Burke was the solicitor who wouldn't help Eva's family and humiliated her mother and Cash exploited his position as a journalist close to the case to abuse Eva's mother. Eva's father handed over the family's life savings to their local police officer, hoping he'd get their son returned to them, but he did nothing and kept all the money.'

Sara nodded. 'Yes, and that copper was Mark Blair, later to become the assistant chief constable.'

'And he was the fourth victim. Then we have the fifth, the minister, Leonard Gibson.'

Sara sighed. 'The whole thing must have been a nightmare for all the families involved, but then for Eva's brother to be placed with Gibson, who abused him, doesn't bear thinking about.'

A noise behind me made me turn towards the community centre, seeing DCI Coe leading Eva into the back of a police car. She smiled at me before ducking her head inside the vehicle.

'Coe must be over the moon,' I said.

'He thinks this will accelerate his climb up the promotional ladder.' She got off the wall. 'He still believes you were involved in the murders, but now we have Cross and Furman in custody, he'll probably leave you alone.'

'Anything to keep him happy and away from me.'

Sara took two steps forward before turning back to me. 'One last thing, Frank.'

'Yeah?'

'Do you think Cross would have done all this if she wasn't dying?'

The wind cut into my scars as I shrugged.

'Who knows how long she's had all this bottled up? She told me she only became aware of everything that happened to her brother when her mother revealed the details on her deathbed, but I'm not so sure.'

'Why?'

I got off the wall. 'You don't plan something as horrific as this, with torture and crucifixions, on the spur of the moment. I'd guess Eva always had suspicions about her brother's suicide, and what her mother told her was the last spark she needed for revenge. Getting Furman's help then set her on this path.'

We stood in silence for thirty seconds.

'What will you do now, Frank?'

I looked at my palm, gazing at what was written there.

'I'll tell you tomorrow.'

The ambulance brought my father home the following morning. He smiled as he arrived, grinning like the Cheshire Cat as I got him inside.

'Where are we going for breakfast, Frank?'

Hunger gripped my stomach. 'Let me make a phone call first, and then you can choose.'

I called social services and arranged for an assessment at the house for three. The old man watched me all the way through the conversation.

'Someone is coming here to see me?'

I explained again what the new situation was going to be. 'Are you okay with that?'

His hands trembled, and I thought it might be a problem until I realised he was moving his fingers to the music on the TV.

'Lydia said it was for the best, and she's a clever young woman. Is she coming with us for breakfast?'

'I'm not sure if she wants to spend her morning with two old blokes, Dad.'

He shook his head, making the wrinkles wobble on his face.

'Watch who you're calling old, Frank. I've still got enough energy to wrestle you to the ground.'

I didn't take him up on that challenge and rang Lydia.

'My father wants to treat you to breakfast,' I said when she answered the phone.

'Great. You can take me to the café on the Coast Road for a full English. Well, I'll drive us there, but you'll pay.'

I agreed with her and the growl in my belly. While waiting for her to arrive, I spoke to the old man about the changes coming to his life.

'As well as helping you around the house, the carers will give me the chance to find a job.'

His eyes glistened. 'Are you going to be a copper again, Frank? People were talking about you in the hospital this morning.'

'Saying what?'

My father thought about it for thirty seconds. 'They said you'd caught a killer and were a hero.' He rubbed at the yellow wrinkles on his cheeks. 'You've always been a hero to me.'

I sat there in shock, my tongue as frozen as my legs. All I could do was change the subject.

'Is Lydia your new best friend, Dad?'

'Did you know her uncle is Tony Thompson?' I nodded. 'She helped me when I had my gambling debts.'

'Helped you how?'

His teeth wobbled as he smiled. 'She stopped Thompson's goons roughing me up.'

This was news to me and something else I was in Lydia's debt for.

'Do you miss the gambling?'

The laugh crawled over his lips. 'Every day I get out of bed is a gamble, Frank.'

I laughed with him as Lydia texted me to say she was outside.

'Walking frame or wheelchair?' I said to the old man.

He got up and brushed the wrinkles from his trousers. 'The stay in the hospital must have done me some good. I'm feeling as fit as a fiddle.'

I looked at him, seeing a musical instrument that needed a lot of tuning.

'Frame it is.'

I helped him out of the house and to the car.

'Morning, Walker and Son,' Lydia said.

The old man grinned as I strapped him into the back and got into the passenger seat.

'You make us sound like Steptoe and Son,' I said.

Lydia laughed. 'That could be a new career for you, Frank – the hippest rag and bone man in the area.'

She drove off, and I switched the radio on, listening to Bowie's *Golden Years* as I replied to her.

'You think I'm hip?'

She gave me a look of mock surprise. 'Damn, is that what I said? I meant to say you'd be the scruffiest rag and bone man around.'

My father snorted laughter as I listened to the music instead of falling for Lydia's baiting. It was good to see both of them happy. Twenty minutes later, we were sitting at an outside table, staring at the sea and waiting for the food to arrive. My dad was talking to a customer's dog.

Lydia leant into me. 'You're okay for people to come into the house four times a day to care for Jack?'

'I don't see any other alternative, Lydia. He needs more help than I can give him, and I have to get a job.'

A server brought our order, and the old man grabbed his bacon sandwich.

Lydia covered her food in tomato sauce. 'That makes two of us.'

'You're looking for work?'

'Yeah. I spent most of my savings buying the flat, so I need to do something soon.' She shovelled the egg into her mouth and grinned at me. 'Maybe we should go into partnership?'

'Like a comedy duo?'

'Or pet walkers'

'We could open a bar on the beach.'

'Or a coffee shop.'

'What about a barbershop?'

She frowned at that notion. 'I don't like the idea of you cutting someone's hair. But, no, I was thinking more about private investigations.'

'You mean the Dire Straits song?'

'Not quite. How about Thompson and Walker Investigations?'

'Why not Walker and Thompson Investigations?'

'We'll have to work on it.'

I bit through a piece of toast, and it warmed my mouth. My dad removed a piece of bacon from his sandwich and gave it to the dog.

'What should we investigate? I don't fancy spying on characters whose partners think they're cheating on them.'

She pondered the question. 'Many crimes aren't investigated, Frank. Sara will tell you how few resources and people the police have. There's a gap there just waiting for us to step into.'

I wasn't sure if she was joking or not. I needed money,

so I required work, and there was only one thing I was good at.

Frank Walker, private investigator.

It didn't fill me full of enthusiasm.

Then I thought of how Kitty Carlisle had given me her mobile phone number last night. I peered at where she'd written it on my palm.

Lydia laughed at me. 'You'll never wash that off, will you?'

For once, I had something to look forward to.

THANK YOU!

Thank you, dear reader for purchasing this book.

If you enjoyed reading about Frank Walker his story continues in these books:

The Frank Walker series
Where The Bodies Are Buried

Many thanks to my wonderful wife for all her support and patience.

Extra special thanks to Karina Gallagher for being a dedicated reader of my work.

Cover design by James, GoOnWrite.com

LYDIA THE TATTOOED LADY

"**L**ydia, the Tattooed Lady**"** is a 1939 song written by Yip Harburg and Harold Arlen. It first appeared in the Marx Brothers movie *At the Circus* (1939) and became one of Groucho Marx's signature tunes.

The song is in the public domain.

ABOUT THE AUTHOR

Andrew French lives amongst faded seaside glamour on the North East coast of England. He likes gin and cats but not together, new music and old movies, curry and ice cream. Slow bike rides and long walks to the pub are his usual exercise, as well as flicking through the pages of good books and the memoirs of bad people.

Find out more at www.andrewsfrench.com

Facebook:

https://www.facebook.com/A-S-French-Author-150145625006018

Twitter:

www.twitter.com/andrewfrench100

Instagram:

www.instagram.com/andrewfrench100

And replies to all his email at mail@andrewsfrench.com

If you have the time, please leave a review at Amazon or Goodreads

Thank you!